DEAD AWAKE: COLLAPSE

ROB ULITSKI

PROLOGUE

Geri settled into bed, the small but tasteful room feeling cosier in low-light. In the daytime, the environment seemed every bit as artificial as it was. Four walls, a suspended ceiling with foam tiles like an office. Scolding bright white lights, buzzing in their fluorescent holders like a trapped wasp.

Her body was plastered with a tangle of different wires, recording her breathing and heart rate and God knew what else. There were so many things attached to her that even a toilet break was a mammoth task, aided by assistants and medical professionals to ensure that the research continued uninterrupted.

Behind the mirrored wall on her left side, the medical team were tracking her every move. Geri knew as much from her initial orientation, where every camera and piece of equipment had been pointed out and explained. It all went over her head a bit, but it was nice for the team to make an effort.

Time moved slowly in this place. There wasn't a clock, which felt weird for the first day or so, then felt kind of freeing.

On the wall opposite, a TV hung from a bracket just a

couple of feet higher than her eyeline. It had been three days so far, and she hadn't felt like using it. There wasn't a huge amount to do in the facility, but she'd kept herself busy reading and documenting her stay in a diary. The first half of her week was phone-free, so it was a chance to catch up on her ever-expanding reading list.

Geri felt like she might finally make it through a whole night of sleep tonight. If it took an arsenal of drugs and tablets and a trashy novel to do so, so be it.

Across the past few days, she'd been prodded and monitored and pumped full of drugs to combat her insomnia. And they had just watched. Through the glass. Through the camera. Geri thought the television might be a psychological trick too, something to watch in case she felt self-conscious.

Geri's eyes fluttered, the unconscious abyss creeping ever closer. More than anything else, she just wanted to dream. She missed the ultra-vibrant stories that used to play out when sleeping wasn't just another impossible chore. She missed her ability to remember even the tiniest detail.

"Okay, I'm ready," she called out to no-one in particular, signalling her wish to rest. Just like that, the last two lights dimmed until darkness fell onto the room. With a deep breath, Geri closed her eyes, and for the first time in recent memory, drifted off without any effort at all.

She dreamt of sunny landscapes and her family, vibrant echoes of her life entwined in a glossy montage.

Then everything went black.

■ ■ ■ ■ ■

She choked and jolted upright, her throat wet and raw. Through milky, sleep-crusted eyes, spotty patterns danced in her vision. Geri couldn't feel her body. She couldn't feel a single thing.

Two doctors hung back in the corner of the room, on-guard and on their feet.

"Geri, stay there. We're going to get some help."

Her eyes felt as if they were being melted from the inside; every sound burrowed into her eardrums.

"Ach. Gest," she spat.

The words wouldn't form. A crimson rage bubbled in Geri's stomach as she ripped wires from her skin in a panicked fit. Her teeth smashed together as she tried to remove the last tangle from her arm, but they wouldn't budge.

"Accch. Heeeelll."

Geri cracked forwards, bent double in her bed. Then, with a painful crunch, her body jostled back against the headboard.

"Dr. Sawyer is coming. She'll help get you back to sleep," one of the doctors croaked.

It was too much to take. The room was closing in on her. Was this all a nightmare? It had to be. Her mind was reeling, a sickly panic pulsating through her body.

Geri thrashed under the covers, before spilling out onto the linoleum floor with a meaty slap. Her eyes were glazed over, jaundiced yellow with bloodshot vessels. From the floor, she began to scratch at the furniture, desperately trying to pull herself back to her feet.

"Heeeelll. Achh… Pleaaa."

Fucking words won't get out of my mouth. I've swallowed them all and now they won't come.

SPLAT.

Geri tripped onto the ground face first, splitting her nose in a violent mash. Shattered bone sliced through her nostril, puncturing the flesh with visceral force.

Need to get out. Need to get out.

Slipping through the pool of blood she'd created, Geri clambered to her feet clumsily, careening into the wall by the

TV. It shook on its brackets, threatening to dismount in the chaos of the situation.

"Please calm down!"

The doctor's voice didn't even sound human anymore. More like growls. An animal. A beast. Geri was trapped, four walls and no space to hide. No place to run. And now, the young man (*Dr Tompkins, she recalled*) was approaching her, arms outstretched.

He wants to seem friendly. He wants to trick me.

He wants to hurt me.

Geri darted towards the nearest exit, catching the edge of the doorframe with her right hip. Her body twisted awkwardly before slamming back to the ground. With a putrid pop, her shoulder tore out of its socket, splintering outwards at a strange angle.

Grunting angrily, Geri pushed hard off of her dislocated arm, lurching forward until she lost balance. A deathly growl rattled from her mouth, and when she was finally back on her feet, it looked as if she'd been mauled by a wild animal.

The hallway was brilliant white for just a moment, until one of the doctors tried to make a move.

Kill. They want to kill me.

Nightmare or not, primal instincts were taking over.

A gloved hand tightened around Geri's shoulder. Before she could even think, two of the fingers were in her mouth, and she was clamping her jaw down to remove them. With a haunting scream and a mouthful of warm fluid, the sickly stumps spurted arcs of blood across the hallway like an abstract art piece, the walls a canvas of viscera. The maimed doctor collapsed to the floor in a wailing heap.

A middle-aged professional stalked out from around the corner, clipboard in hand. She was in a business suit, hair tied back in a neat ponytail. Geri let out another guttural groan as tears began to run down her face. The gruff utterances turned into weeping sobs, Geri's body frozen in a defensive stance.

For just a moment, she looked like a lost child, her mind broken and confused. Milky eyes reflected a universe of emotions.

"Geri. It's Dr. Sawyer. We need to get you back to your room."

"Helhelhelhelpppp," the words twisted in Geri's mouth, dry saliva beading at the corners.

Dr. Sawyer stretched out her right hand, manicured red nails reflecting the fluorescents above.

Need to go. Go. Go. Go.

SLAM.

Geri burst into a frantic sprint, directed right at the nearest wall, seemingly unaware of its design. Her nose was halfway torn off now, the left half grappling with strands of sinew to keep her face together. The front of her hospital gown oozed with a miscellany of bodily fluid, stained a stale purple-red.

Dr. Sawyer withdrew a small radio from her belt.

"Lock down elevator B12. Clear the stairway."

Most of the team had retreated to a different room, whilst a distorted siren signalled the lockdown procedure. The hallway absorbed the vibrant emergency lights, coruscating in looping patterns, highlighting the organic red matter spread around the space.

Geri grappled with another doctor, and before Dr. Sawyer could make sense of the situation, the patient ripped the man's throat out with her teeth, uninhibited bloodlust taking over her being. Dr. Sawyer had never expected anything like this to happen. Not at this facility. Not under her care. Their worst case scenario had come true, and at the worst possible time. It was too late to change things now.

With a deafening screech, Geri carved a jagged slash across the male doctor's face with her nails before slamming him so hard into the wall his spinal cord cracked, jutting through his already mangled throat cavity.

It was all moving too fast. Security was nowhere near the floor. Dr. Sawyer had to act.

"Please take a deep breath."

The broken woman faced a large window at the end of the hallway. Her limbs were twisted and misshapen, stained blotchy red and white. Some kind of prickly rash contoured around her neck and face, spread in a pinprick pattern.

With jittery, fractured movements, Geri turned to face Dr. Sawyer, her face warped in terrified shock. As if frozen mid-scream, her mouth was stretched into a wide, unnatural shape, eyes wide and pleading. Dr. Sawyer tried to speak, but was interrupted by a growl booming from the depths of Geri's core.

Instead of sprinting towards the doctor, Geri turned back to the window, hurtling herself at the mirrored glass. The initial impact shook the frame, but the structure didn't budge. In sickening delight, Geri cackled, stumbling back to put some distance between herself and the wall.

Moments later, her body was a blur of white and red as the pane cracked into a glistening spider web, imploding . Fragments of flesh and fabric clung to protruding shards as the rest of Geri free-falled into the atmosphere. A juicy thud outside signalled the end of her journey, a pile of blown-out organs and patchwork skin.

Dr. Sawyer looked down at the gory scene, fingers wrapped around her radio. A glitchy voice fought its way through the static.

"Dr. Sawyer. Do you have any updates?"

"Get me Oswald."

DAY 1

DAY 1

CHAPTER 1
ALICE

Alice should have found the money to take the train instead. She lamented her prior travel decisions whilst cramped in the back corner of a commuter coach, the twice-a-day service from London Victoria to Egglemore Parkway. A low hum of chatter permeated the carriage, an amalgam of workers and tourists, their voices sporadically interrupted by on-board tannoy announcements. The same cycle of instructions on a loop: *don't smoke, don't drink, don't eat.* But in that corporate-polite tone Alice had grown used to in her career as a journalist.

The space was stuffy, a heavy cloud of body odour and stale breakfast items lingering at head height. She snatched a face mask from her handbag, snapped the strap around her ears, and took a deep, stifled breath. Her eyes traced the coach, sizing up her fellow passengers, painting a mental picture of their lives and adventures and reasons for travelling. How many of them had as important a reason as Alice to be on this journey? Probably none.

A dozen or so students were dotted around the carriage, their youthfully optimistic faces and overstuffed backpacks giving them away. It was the start of the new university year, and Alice could bet on them being freshers. Excitement radiated from each one, the promise of late-night parties, social events, and drunken hook-ups burning brightly on the horizon.

Alice could really use a cigarette. Maybe something stronger. A nap would have to suffice.

Her eyes were barely closed before the tannoy crackled, leaving a few seconds of dead air before continuing with the loop of instructions.

"Can't ever sleep on these, darling," the man next to her interrupted. His face was sweaty, beads of saltwater dripping from his brow onto vintage-looking frames.

"Ah, okay," Alice started. "Well, I'm gonna try anyway. Enjoy your journey."

The man ignored her tactful dismissal, and hacked up some phlegm, ready to talk again.

"I've taken this route for five years. Guess how many times I've slept?"

Alice gently screwed her face up, trying to hide her disdain.

"I don't know. Zero?"

"Well, about three times. Five years is a while, you know. But the odds aren't in your favour, that's what I'm saying."

As he talked, Alice could feel his body encroaching on her side of the chair divide. His shoulder was fighting for purchase, edging its way behind hers.

"Well. Thanks for the chat. I'm going to sleep now."

Before he had a chance to speak up again, Alice popped in her earbuds, and turned to face the window. Any protests to her attitude would have to fight for attention against some noughties heavy metal. She grabbed a small bottle of hand sanitiser from her bag and cleaned her hands.

A blur of grey buildings whipped past the window as the pastel sunrise faded into the clouds. Alice's mind was on Egglemore, and the dichotomous relationship she had with the coastal city. In many ways, it reminded her of London. Lots of people. Opportunities if you're in the right industry (e.g. pharmaceuticals or tech). It also had a dark underbelly, a network of nightmares bubbling under the surface, just waiting to burrow out and bloom into disaster.

It's the reason she'd spent so much time away from her hometown. The connections you have to the place you're born are like foundations, in some ways. If they're built correctly, your foundations can prop you up for life, give you the ability to stand strong and weather the storms as they rain down. But if they're uneven or worse, incomplete, it's only a matter of time until those cracks start to show.

Alice didn't like to think of her foundations. They were intrinsically linked to Egglemore, and heading back felt like excavating her own life from the inside out.

"Always running ten minutes late. Why can't these things keep to time?"

In the silent transition between songs, Alice could hear her talkative neighbour continue to complain, even without an audience. Three minutes of his chatter felt like an hour had passed. She couldn't bear to imagine the toll a whole journey's worth would take. The heaviest metal wasn't going to drown out his droning.

Flitting between silence or violence, Alice chose the middle road. A polite request. Popping out her right earbud with pinched fingers, she turned to the man with a radiant smile.

"I'm not used to being up this early, and have an important meeting at the other end. Would you mind if I kept to myself for a bit, and perhaps we could talk later?"

The man stared at her for a few moments, brow furrowed in confusion. Any optimism Alice had was soon snuffed out by another round of whining, on everything from timetables to young people to the state of the economy, topics upon topics piled into bursts of breathless word vomit. Alice checked out mentally, her gaze drifting back to the front of the bus, where two athletic twenty-somethings sat in sportswear, on the way to a tournament or competition perhaps.

Something in their mannerisms caught Alice's attention. When she'd seen them embark, they'd been laughing and joking, two kids on an adventure. But now, the one in the window seat (Blonde Hair) was acting erratically, lunging at the spotlight above him. His fingers poked at the switch, illuminating the lamp in a frenzied pattern. His friend, (Brown Hair), was trying to settle him down, pulling on his arms and restraining him to his seat.

"Stop it mate. What are you doing?"

Most passengers probably saw them as two young men mucking around, breezing through the trip with a bit of harmless horseplay. But when you'd met as many people as Alice had, often under constraints of time or conflict, you developed an eye for the little clues. The anguish in Brown Hair's movements. A sense of escalating tension. Blonde Hair's relentless focus on the light above them, a fascinating obsession inconsistent with usual daily patterns.

"You're gonna get us kicked off, what the fuck?"

The rest of the coach had caught onto the conflict now, silent gasps and swallowed utterances dancing in the air.

"Can someone help me?" Brown Hair choked, as Blonde Hair convulsed in his place, limbs flailing. Brown Hair was squatting in his chair now, engrossed in his friend's condition but completely prepared to exit *stage left* on a moment's notice.

The loudmouth next to Alice was silent for the first time on the journey, but she'd already tuned him out. Her focus was locked on the two young men, and the innate feeling that something was about to go terribly wrong.

CHAPTER 2

TODD

The estate looked peaceful in the morning. In contrast to the ageing, brutalist tower blocks, a scattering of orange leaves were strewn across the courtyard, covered in a layer of autumn frost.

Four imposing structures faced in on the courtyard, each housing hundreds of residents. Generations of families had lived in these walls, and Todd found a certain sense of comfort in the community that surrounded him. His apartment was on the third floor, only a fraction of the way up the twenty stories each building comprised.

His early morning routine was built around peace and mindfulness. Whenever he wasn't journaling his thoughts or practising a new yoga pose (which, at 6′ 5″, came with its own restrictions—especially in his box room) he liked to set up his drone and take a breezy journey through the outside world.

The drone was a near-silent model to avoid disturbing the neighbours. Every now and then, he'd get a twitch at the curtains or a baffled-looking stare from a resident, but most of them had just gotten used to his hobby. That, or they didn't care too much.

From his room, Todd navigated the vehicle with a robust-looking remote and a slick white headset. In a practised routine, he gently thumbed the controls, whilst his goggles displayed a high definition live feed from the camera. He explored for ten minutes or so before setting the drone to recall, retrieving it from a ledge outside his window. It all seemed peaceful out there, another normal day. As good as any for a little fresh air.

The agenda for the day started at the pharmacy, then to the supermarket and back home. Todd had calculated the journey would take approximately half an hour without stopping to chat to anyone, probably closer to forty minutes if he was being realistic. Both places opened at 8:00am, giving him fifteen minutes to venture down to ground level and walk over.

If he caught the pharmacy first, he'd be just in time for the fresh bread at the shop, which would score him points with his Gran. It also left the least amount of room for unexpected social situations, given everyone would be sleeping or getting ready for work.

With his mind racing with mantras to remind him to breathe, Todd grabbed his backpack and stuffed it with a handful of carrier bags. He reached out to the handle and took a moment. The metal was cold in his hands, caressed by a gentle breeze filtering through a gap in the doorframe.

Todd focused on his ideal scenario. He'd spent the morning scoping out the area, playing the journey through his mind a dozen times. Two places to visit then right back home in under an hour. A simple, everyday trip. If only he could make these things feel everyday.

Todd pushed down on the handle and opened the front door hesitantly. He rushed to turn as soon as he closed the door and counted down his steps to the elevator. The elevator was out of order, quite unsurprisingly, so a backup plan was already forming in Todd's head.

Ten flights of stairs will add five minutes or so, so that's not the end of the world...

He tried not to ruminate on it too much, and quickly descended the staircase to keep to the timings in his head.

Todd reached the pharmacy with a few minutes to spare, so waited patiently until the dim neon sign sputtered to life. A few residents followed him in and formed a queue, thankfully possessing the manners to keep their distance. There was nothing worse than someone being right up against you in a queue, jostling for their place with all the decorum of a wrecking ball.

Todd took a few deep breaths and grounded himself in the moment, allowing himself to feel the emotions as they came. The counter was unmanned, which gave him a couple of minutes to get his thoughts together. He took the prescription from his pocket and neatly unfolded it, flattening the bend marks against his jeans. Reading under his breath, he rehearsed what he was going to say over and over, placing undue emphasis on every word and the gesture that would match it.

"Hi, can I help?" asked a stocky brunette woman behind the counter. Todd cleared his throat and handed the prescription to the clerk, hoping she didn't notice how wet and sweaty his palms were.

"Hi. Prescription for Mrs Daniels please. Thank you."

Todd smiled, and painfully counted down the seconds until she reacted like he'd hoped.

"Two minutes. Feel free to sit."

The woman gestured towards a row of three hard plastic chairs, and Todd thanked her just a moment too late, cutting into the conversation of the next person in line.

"Sorry, was there something else?" the clerk asked. Todd shook his head awkwardly and shuffled over to the seat. He squatted down on the chair, the unusual contour prodding his thighs. Nervously, he started tapping his foot and shaking his leg, his whole body moist. Todd's heart fluttered in rippling waves, immune to the deep breathing technique he was trying to distract himself with.

At the front entrance, a skinny elderly man ambled through the door, introduced by a digital doorbell. The tinny sound caught Todd's attention, and his mood settled instantly.

It was Benjamin from 132a. Benjamin stood around six feet tall, his thinning hair swept into a tidy style. Wearing a red cardigan and cream corduroy trousers, he looked in good spirits. As soon as he saw Todd, his face beamed, and he cut around the queue to come and say hi.

Todd matched his jolly energy, putting aside his discomfort for a moment.

"Benjamin! How've you been?"

"Great as always, Todd. How is your Gran? How are you?"

Todd smiled. It was no secret that Benjamin and his Gran were close friends; they'd both lived on the estate their whole lives. When Todd's Grandad died, Benjamin was the first one round to comfort her, and he'd made weekly visits ever since.

"Good, all good, thanks. Still coming over this afternoon? She's been planning her outfit all week."

Benjamin nodded, wiping his nose with a handkerchief.

"I wouldn't miss it for the world."

His face was lit up like a teenager. It had taken the best part of a year, but Todd had finally organised a date between Benjamin and his Gran. Their friendship had always had an essence of longing and desire, but it was never the right timing. Now they were both single, ready to mingle, and quite bluntly running out of time to enjoy themselves, so Todd decided to act.

"She's making you her lasagne, I think. It's ten out of ten, not even just saying that. I wouldn't recommend wearing white, though. I've ruined countless tops with that sauce."

Todd was word-spewing again. He gently reminded himself to slow down.

"Well, I'll look forward to it. I'll be over at 3:00pm, if that's okay?"

Todd nodded just as the clerk called his name for the prescription.

"I better get that. See you in a bit, Mr Oakes."

Todd swung by the clerk to grab the paper package and filed past the line to the door. He swung it open, greeted by the annoying bell, and stepped onto the footpath.

A wailing screech cackled from a pair of teenagers, who zoomed past on an e-scooter, two bodies grappling to stay on the vehicle. Todd stopped in his tracks, inwardly swearing at the kids. They were only having a laugh, but loud noises were not part of Todd's plan today, and he'd already had more than enough of the outside world.

He watched them disappear into the distance, their silhouettes vanishing into the murky shadow of the buildings as they passed. Then, Todd rehearsed a mantra in his head and started walking, eager to get to the supermarket and back into the warm apartment.

CHAPTER 3

MAGGIE

"Look, I know you can't hear well right now, but don't just blank me when I'm talking to you."

Maggie snatched the gearstick, struggling to reach the speed limit. She'd driven the blue Ford Focus for almost a decade, a fortieth birthday present from a friend, and though it sputtered and struggled to drive more than a few miles on most days, it was the best car she'd ever owned. Just don't ask it to go over fifty miles an hour on a hill. In fact, it was probably best to avoid hills altogether.

In the backseat, her daughter Claire was sulking, teenage emotions manifesting in eye rolls and deep, pained sighs. Maggie's eyes were on the road, her shoulder-length ginger hair neatly tucked behind her ears. She could hear every groan, tut, and click of Claire's tongue. For what it was worth, Claire couldn't hear much at all, so her exaggerated gestures might have been compensating for that.

"We'll know more after seeing the doctor. I'm sure we'll get it sorted."

Maggie was impressed. She almost believed her own words.

Last December, Claire woke up completely deaf in her left

ear. Less than twelve months later, her right ear was following suit, albeit at a slower rate. They'd been messed around with cancelled appointments and endless rescheduling, but the day had finally come to see a specialist, and that meant a trip to Egglemore.

"Can you turn this one up?" Claire asked, gesturing towards the radio. Though it was blasting out at a volume loud enough to pop your head, Maggie wanted to be empathetic. She cranked the dial and flicked her hair back over her ears, providing as much of a buffer as possible between the music and the last shreds of her sanity. At least it put a smile back on Claire's face.

BEEEEEEEEPP.

A minivan swerved into her lane from the right side, nearly clipping her bumper. Maggie reflexively hit the horn, compressing it for a few seconds to make her frustration known.

"Fucking idiot! Dickhead!"

Claire was cracking up in the backseat, entertained by Maggie's *one to a hundred* approach.

"They can't hear you, Mum."

Maggie scoffed, her heart rate finally descending back to where it should be.

"You wanna bet on that?"

She honked the horn again for good measure, finally able to pass when the vehicle cruised back to its original position. Curious, Maggie took a glance over at the driver of the van, wondering what kind of person would be so erratic on the road. She wasn't one to pre-judge, but if she saw another tiny elderly woman trying to drive without even being able to see over the dashboard, she'd have to call the police.

But it wasn't an elderly woman. Quite the opposite, in fact. A young man, no older than mid-twenties. His mouth was warped in a panicked cry. The female in the passenger seat looked like she was attacking him.

Maggie didn't dare look for too long, not with Claire in the back. She had to be a responsible driver herself, and lock in on the road. But the chaos in that vehicle was endangering everyone. Its wheels edged over the lane marking before a hasty correction set it back on course. Maggie could hear the gears grinding. Smoke plumed from the exhaust.

"Mum? What's going on?"

Maggie flicked on her indicators, observing the passenger-side wing mirror. A steady stroll of vehicles ambled past her car, unaware of the disruption unfolding in the other lane. She needed to find a gap in the traffic to put some distance between them and the other vehicle.

"Call the police, honey. Explain that—"

"I can't hear you,"

Maggie bit her lip, taking her frustration out on the horn.

"Fuck me can someone just make a space for—"

The shrill screams of the gearbox outside grew louder, and the minivan took a hard left, swerving in front of Maggie and the adjacent lane. With escalating speed, the vehicle careened over to the slip road, and took the exit. In her rearview mirror, she could see the van screech into the distance, enveloped in a cloud of muddy smoke.

"Are they okay?" Claire gasped. Maggie didn't know the answer to that question. But she couldn't in good conscience go ahead without alerting someone.

"I'm gonna pull over. One second."

Cautiously navigating the stream of traffic beside her, Maggie indicated and slid the car into the nearside lane, and then onto the hard shoulder. The car coasted to a stop and Maggie switched off the engine.

"Okay, listen..." Maggie started, turning so Claire could read her lips. "Under no circumstances do you get out of this car. It's dangerous. Okay?"

Claire nodded, her bad attitude dissipating.

"Okay. I'll just be a sec."

Maggie turned back and opened her door, carefully regarding the hurtling flow of cars mere inches away. With her back flat against the frame of the vehicle, she sidestepped around to the rear and tried her best to look back for any sign of the minivan. The slip road was hidden behind a thicket of overgrown bushes, and there were no immediate signs of concern. No smoke, no burning smell in the air.

Maggie grabbed her phone from her pocket and dialled the emergency services.

"Hello. Police, please. Maybe an ambulance."

She held for a beat.

"Hello. My name is Margaret Bunton. I'm pulled up on the side of the M29. Right around junction five… Okay, well I witnessed a dangerous driving incident a few minutes ago. The passenger was attacking the man, and… yes. They took the exit towards Chesterton Valley. Yes. Okay. Okay. Thank you."

Maggie ended the call and turned around, aghast to see Claire outside and leaning on the boot, texting on her phone.

"Excuse me?"

Maggie clapped, a thunderous roar to get Claire's attention.

"What?" Claire groaned.

"These cars are going seventy miles an hour. If one of them hits you, how far do you think I'll have to go to collect all of your limbs?"

"Fine, I'll get back in."

Claire headed back towards the traffic. Maggie clapped again.

"NO CLAIRE! Other side. You can crawl back to your seat."

"Fine," she sighed, opening the passenger side door. She awkwardly manoeuvred across the back seat and into her place. Maggie scowled, scaling the perimeter of the car until she was back inside, safe from the chaotic motorway.

She twisted the key in the engine and it roared to life. Several decorative charms rattled against the plastic panel, a delicate symphony of jingles.

"I'm sorry," Claire groaned. Maggie pulled the car into gear, and set off.

"It's okay. Don't worry."

Slipping out from the hard shoulder, Maggie carefully timed her speed to slot between the never-ending assembly line of cars.

"Mum? I said I'm sorry."

"It's okay. Just don't do it again," she mumbled, eyes on the road.

"Now who's blanking who?" Claire squealed, getting irate. Maggie's eyes shot to the rearview, and she lifted her face slightly, allowing Claire to see her lips.

"Okay! I've just said okay. Don't worry. Jesus."

She patted her hand on the front passenger seat and snatched a handful of sweets. Rather ungraciously, she twisted her arm to pass them to her daughter, before giving up and chucking them to her.

"Eat those and give my ears a break."

Claire smiled warmly, unwrapping one of the sweets. Hopefully, Maggie prayed, it would be enough to keep her quiet for the rest of the journey.

CHAPTER 4

ALICE

"What's going on back there?"

The driver was exasperated, his eyes flitting between the monitor at the front of the coach and the road out in front of him. The boys were directly behind his seat, blocked by a fabric partition, so he couldn't get a good look at them.

A voice erupted on the tannoy. Alice could see the radio in the driver's hand, shaking nervously as he tried to control the situation.

"Can everyone return to their seats and strap in. The next service station is in ten miles. We will make an emergency stop."

The vehicle jolted forwards, ramping up in speed, before returning to its normal pace. Blonde Hair was on his feet, babbling out loud, flailing like a cornered animal. Brown Hair was in the aisle, shielding himself from his friend with his backpack.

"Acch.. Fuucckking. Get awaaayyy."

Alice was engrossed in the conflict, which grew louder and more violent with each passing moment. The man next to her was glued to his phone, recording the pair with a smirk on his face.

"Look at these two! It's not even midday and they're drunk!"

The man launched a plosive spittle over his screen, beads of saliva pooling around his thumb. That turned Alice's stomach, and she wished more than anything that he'd just move seats.

"JAKE DON'T!"

Ripping her from her thoughts, Alice looked back just in time to see Blonde Hair smash his head into the window. The heavy *clunk* reverberated through the coach, and even from this distance, she could see residue from his face on the glass. Frantically, the boy launched an attack with his elbows and fists, seemingly disturbed by his own reflection.

Brown Hair was at the front, pleading with the driver to stop the coach. The other passengers were rigid with fear, cemented to their chairs in complete disbelief. Blonde Hair propped one leg on the chair and attempted to jump at the glass. He bounced off in an almost comedic manner, leaving only a Rorschach stain of blood behind.

The tannoy kicked in again.

"If there are any police officers or security personnel on board, please make yourself known to the driver."

Piercing screams echoed from the front as Blonde Hair directed his attention towards his fellow passengers. A young girl was already sprinting to the back, her instincts coming into play. Alice stood up, concerned that the situation was quickly becoming untenable.

"Fuuuuckkking. Acccch. Helllllp."

The boy hacked up a torrent of crimson vomit, his voice choking through pained sobs. His mouth locked open into a twisted, inhuman shape as tears gushed from milky yellow eyes. Without warning, he burst towards an older man across the aisle, launching at him with the brutality of a feral animal. Alice caught a glimpse of the driver at the front, and before she knew it, the steering wheel twisted right then left, aggressively rocking the vehicle to the side.

Blonde Hair's fingers were twisted in the man's hair, tugging at his scalp as if defeathering a chicken. The motion of the coach sent him flying back to the floor, taking a tangle of grey locks with him. The old man shrieked, patting viscous blood from his scalp. The lady to his left—his wife, perhaps—quickly rose from her seat, tending to his wounds with a decorative handkerchief.

Blonde Hair cracked up into a seated position, and though Alice could only see the top half of his body from her vantage point, it was evident that he was now chewing on the man's thin hair, shovelling the strands in his mouth like a toddler. It was disgusting, and the other passengers seemed to agree, expressing their revulsion with silent whispers and swallowed gagging sounds.

The coach trembled as the driver took a hard left onto the slip road. Blonde Hair slid violently across the aisle, colliding with Brown Hair, sending him right to the ground. The pair grappled on the floor, exchanging hard blows in a valiant attempt to destroy the other. Brown Hair slammed his fist hard into Blonde Hair's nose, cracking the bone in one blow. It was enough to break his friend's grip, and he quickly tugged himself back to a standing position.

"Please, Jake. What's wrong with you?"

Several passengers tried to rise from their seats, but were quickly discarded back into them by the momentum of the vehicle. The driver careened around a sharp bend and compressed the accelerator on the final stretch towards the service station. Alice heard one of the front wheels blow out and the driver quickly snatched the radio from his dashboard.

"Brace for impact."

With that, the driver smacked the horn, compressing it right until the last moment. A gaggle of people in the car park dispersed quickly, leaving room for the runaway coach.

Brown Hair dove back into his seat just as Blonde Hair gained his footing.

SMASSSSSH.

A cacophony of crunching and shattered glass boomed on impact, lifting the back of the coach from its wheels. Blonde Hair flew through the carriage, getting a few seconds of airtime before smashing into the windscreen, his body forced through the glass in a grotesque crush.

They had hit some kind of short concrete bollard, which completely obliterated the bumper. Blood stained the front of the carriage, fragments of flesh and bone glued to the interior.

"Is everyone okay?" the driver asked.

An awkward silence hung in the air. How were they meant to answer that question?

Alice released her seatbelt, fumbling with the mechanism until she was completely free. Twisting in her seat, she wiggled her legs and arms, checking she hadn't sustained any injuries. Everything seemed to be in working order, aside from a growing pressure in her head.

"I have a football match at 5:00pm! What am I meant to do now?" the man beside her groaned, his priorities at odds with the situation. Alice had her own plans and timeline to stick to, but she wasn't running her mouth with selfish tirades.

"Are you joking right now?" she questioned, her face completely stoic.

"What?"

"We just crashed. That boy went through the windscreen."

Brown Hair was already at the door, phone to his ear as he tried to get off the vehicle.

"I need to call an ambulance! Let me off. I need to see if he's okay!" The boy looked younger, more innocent in the light of day. "Open this door now!"

The man by her side groaned again, pulling her back into the disagreement.

"I haven't seen my team play in two years. Who's going to refund my tickets if I don't make it now?"

Alice rolled her eyes, trying her best to hold her tongue.

"Tell you what. How about you worry about that when we're inside?"

"Who do you think you're talking to, little girl?" he spat.

That was the last straw.

As the driver turned off the engine, passengers gathered their things and formed an orderly queue in the carriage. Alice turned to fully face the man.

"I think I'm *talking to* an unwashed slob who cares more about some fucking sports match then the safety of these passengers."

The man tried to interject. Alice didn't let him.

"I think I'm *talking to* some nobody whose head is filled with so many stupid thoughts, they all rush out every time you open that fat mouth of yours. And I'm done. I've been polite, I've been quiet, now I'm telling you to shut the fuck up and keep your distance before I really give you something to moan about."

Alice pushed her way past the man, dragging her over-shoulder bag across his body, and joined the queue. With a final word to say, she arched her head back at him.

"And if you dare try and cause trouble when we're inside, I'll make sure that you never get to see another football match again in your pointless life."

The queue started to amble forwards, and Alice followed behind, right into the daylight.

CHAPTER 5
CHARLES

It was going to be another beautiful day—Charles could feel it. The weather stayed chillingly crisp from dusk till dawn nowadays, heading into winter, but that wouldn't take any of the magic away from another twenty-four hours on planet Earth.

There were things that could make it better, of course. A hot shower. A friendly interaction. Getting back to his makeshift tent without it being destroyed or vandalised. A life on the streets was no mean feat, but Charles thrived on the miscellany of the everyday.

Charles grabbed his personal CD player from the vintage brown messenger bag hanging over his shoulder and unravelled the wired earbuds. He'd had both items for well over five years, but they worked just as well as the day he was given them.

It was a young, brunette girl who had bought them for him, a stranger on a mission to make someone's day a little bit brighter. From talking to her, she was a student at Egglemore University, a music major, and was rifling around the record shop one random Monday at the same time as him. He liked to browse through the shop's collection anytime he was in the area, and though he didn't have the money to buy anything himself, he always imagined walking out with lots of new music to discover.

The girl would've known almost instantly that Charles was homeless—his clothes and battle scars from the streets gave that away. But she didn't let any prejudice hold her back from a delightful conversation, on everything from classical music to noughties pop. The gift was a parting gesture, and Charles had held onto the memory warmly ever since.

He hoped to bump into her again someday, to give him an opportunity to pay her back. The Charles of today was pretty much the same as the one in that music shop five years ago, but with a better mindset and outlook on life. His life had been full of serendipitous moments with strangers, and it was his mission to pay back every single act of kindness, in whatever way he could.

The CD of choice this cold Wednesday lunchtime was *Now That's What I Call Music! 1999,* a brilliant compilation disk from the turn of the century. It was a personal favourite, boasting hits such as Lenny Kravitz's *Fly Away* and *Flat Beat* by Mr Oizo. As the first track started filtering through the earbuds, a sense of serene calm washed over Charles's body.

It was going to be a great day. He was even more sure of it now.

Charles sauntered down the high street, catching his reflection in every passing window. It was pretty quiet for a Wednesday; usually the bars and eateries were packed full of local workers. The surrounding buildings were mostly offices or retail, a mile or so out from the main tech hub. As he paced through the shadows of the imposing structures, a mish-mash of modern and old Victorian renovations, he decided to refamiliarise himself with his mission for the day.

From the same weathered messenger bag, he grabbed a thick, leatherbound notebook, imprinted with the initials CM. He'd owned this book his entire adult life, and its vintage was apparent from the yellowed pages and water-marked edges. Charles opened the book in the middle, and slid out the book ribbon. He walked to the beat of Texas's *Summer Sun* as he scanned the pages, memorising the scribbled-down information.

NAME: Jeanette

DATE: 12/12/21

LOCATION: Turtle Avenue

LOOKS: Brunette. Medium build. Frumpy clothes. Slightly upturned nose. Blue eyes. Mole just above her lip.

Bought me a coffee and pastry from Greggs. Wouldn't accept any change for it.

Charles made these notes after every act of kindness, no matter how small or seemingly insignificant. From a passing smile to giving him food, it all went in the book, ready to be repaid when fate felt it opportune.

He couldn't quite picture Jeanette the brunette, but knew the little details would come in handy when he saw her again. *Fate leads the way*, that's what he always thought.

Sometimes, Charles would bump into someone completely different on his daily quest. A person's silhouette might jolt his memory, a voice might stop him in his tracks. As long as his focus was on intention and gratitude, he'd be well on his way to reconnecting with these beautiful souls.

Last week, he'd bumped into a woman that fit his description of Jeanette down to the last detail. Something about her had felt familiar, and it wasn't until he'd tracked down another stranger that his mind connected the dots. It took a couple of hours to rifle through his notebook that night, but he eventually stumbled upon the entry, and it just clicked.

By the time Charles reached Betty's Bakery, a quaint eatery adjacent to Turtle Avenue, the time was 13:01pm. He'd seen *potential Jeanette* sipping a latté in the doorway last week around the same time, perched halfway on the street and halfway in the establishment. Judging by her body language, she was busy chatting, and radiated a kind energy.

Charles set down his bag and crouched down onto the pavement, crossing his legs patiently. From his perspective, he could see people walking in and out of the café, and if *potential Jeanette* walked on by, he'd give her a gift. He couldn't afford one of the fancy lattés, so that was off the table. But his gifts were rarely monetary in value, anyway.

He tore a page from the back of the notebook and grabbed a blunt pencil, then started sketching the bakery. From the ornate window frames through to the curious way the sun's rays reflected in the glass, every detail was an opportunity to capture the moment, and he revelled in the process. Not a moment after he signed the drawing, *potential Jeanette* rocked up in a long grey coat and baggy jeans.

She was mid-30s, if that, and despite a questionable proximity to good fashion sense, joy seemed to envelop her being. Charles could see her at the counter, and timed his approach to arrive at the door just as she was leaving.

"Excuse me, miss. I drew this for you."

Charles handed over the drawing, and the woman's face beamed as she took a look.

"You just made this?"

"I did. You have a warm energy, and I think you're a good person. So I made this."

"Can I hug you? Oh my god that's so nice."

Jeanette pulled Charles in for a hug, and was polite enough not to recoil in horror at his scent. It had been a few days since he showered or washed his clothes. There was no doubt about the smell. Lovely lady.

"I'm actually just on lunch so I have to go, but see you around maybe? Thank you again, I'm going to show all my colleagues."

Charles nodded and gave her a polite wave. As she disappeared over the horizon, he grabbed his notepad and crossed her name from the list.

The wind was picking up a bit, so it was the perfect time to grab a coffee. Charles had an old friend just around the corner, a middle-aged gentleman who used to share the same patch on the high street. He'd been off the streets for the best part of ten years, but was always more than happy to offer a coffee and a hot meal if Charles was on that side of town.

His friend made the best sandwiches; Charles could hardly wait. The day was proving itself to be just as good as he had imagined.

CHAPTER 6
TODD

Todd had been teaching this client for well over a year and still got nervous sweats a few minutes before the call. The video software covered the whole 42″ monitor in front of him, and the mouse was already poised to hit *call*.

He was freshly dressed in one of the ten identical gym outfits he owned, colour-matched to his bedroom walls (light blue) and the logo for his remote personal training business (a slightly darker light blue).

2 minutes to go.

The plan for the session was already loaded on-screen, hidden behind the current display. Usually running about forty-five minutes, most of his clients favoured a short warmup *(ten minutes)*, cardio *(twenty minutes)*, stretching *(ten minutes)*, and cool down *(five minutes)*. That was the plan today. Nothing off-track there.

But this client had a habit of running late. A few minutes, give or take, but that was enough to throw the whole day into disarray.

1 minute to go.

A shift of a few minutes could easily become an hour or so across the day. Todd didn't like the process of apologising for his lateness to the rest of the day's clients, especially when his own timekeeping was one of his best traits.

Call.

Todd clicked his mouse, and a smaller dialogue box opened on-screen. A text overlay popped up onto screen, and a few moments later, a middle-aged woman greeted him with a smile. Todd exhaled, letting out a build-up of nervous energy, and felt ready to start the session.

"Hey Joan. How are you?"

"Good, good," the woman replied. "Had a bit of a tumble earlier but still ready to go."

"Oh I'm sorry to hear that," Todd said, noticing the abrasions on her cheek and arm. "Do let me know if you need to skip any parts today: we can work around you."

Joan smiled.

"Can never tell what kind of nutters are gonna be around can you? Knocked me right off my bike, this man did. Crying and screaming bloody murder. Must be something in the water."

Todd continued with the small talk for another thirty seconds or so, then segued into the session. His timings waited for no one.

Towards the end of the timeslot, Joan seemed irritated. She kept losing focus, turning her head away slightly as if observing something in the distance. Todd was far too shy to dare to ask what was distracting her, but a few moments later Joan spelled it out.

"There's someone at the door. He won't stop knocking. Do you mind if I—?"

She pointed off-screen, presumably at the door.

"Go ahead, please."

The woman stood up and walked away from the camera, leaving a blank, mustard-yellow wall in the background. Todd tapped his fingers on the desk gently, rehearsing the rest of the session in his mind. With a deep clatter and an off-pitch shriek, a blur of silhouettes dashed past the camera. The table shifted, Joan's laptop clattering on the surface.

"Joan? Are you alright?"

Before any more of the scene revealed itself, the laptop toppled to the floor, and Joan's camera went blank.

"Joan?"

KNOCK KNOCK.

Todd's soul damn near jumped out of his body. He turned. The door swung open slightly, a shaky hand clinging to the doorknob. It was Todd's Gran, dressed in a lovely emerald shirt and black trousers. She looked sophisticated and upstanding—two words that didn't often accompany the woman. Not that Todd would ever dare say that to her face. He probably wouldn't even say it out loud.

"Can you do my necklace, love? I can't get the clasp."

Todd stood up. He would get in touch with Joan later in the day. She had young Grandchildren and two dogs at the property, she'd once explained, so it was probably just a prank of some kind.

"Come sit here, then," Todd said, offering his chair.

His Gran passed him the necklace, and plonked down on the chair, her bony frame thudding against the seat. Todd pulled back the clasp with his fingernail and gently fastened it around her neck, sifting her hair back over the chain.

"There we are. Ready to go. Now what time is it?" Todd asked.

"2:00pm. An hour early, but I need to do some more prep in the kitchen, anyway."

Todd nodded and helped her up from the seat.

"Don't forget to save me some. I can't just sit and watch someone eat my portion."

His Gran rolled her eyes, patting him on the shoulder.

"Now when have I ever left you out, Toddy?"

That was a fair point. The answer was never.

"Alright then, get going. Don't want to run down the clock."

She turned to leave the room, adjusting the necklace to her taste.

"Oh, and Gran... put the kettle on if you're going past it."

"Cheeky bugger," she groaned, before pulling the door closed.

"Don't forget the sugar!" he joked, before turning back to the desktop. Joan's camera was still blank. Her allotted time was up, but he felt uneasy about ending the call. There was an anxious bubbling in Todd's stomach, a strong sense that something had happened to her. He knew it was probably just a case of overactive imagination, the truth far more dull than the colourful catastrophes in his head.

After two attempts at trying to call her back, he wrapped up the call and sent her an email. Joan hadn't ever shared a phone number, nor an address or any identifying information. There was no reason to. So he was left with two options: go about his day, or call the police.

He might have been concerned, but he definitely wasn't *call the police* concerned. Plus, where would he tell them to go?

So he shut down the software and grabbed a bottle of water from a small minifridge in the corner of the box room. After gulping down half the contents, he squatted on the floor, awkwardly manoeuvring his lanky frame into a crossed-leg position.

When his body was adequately positioned, knees rammed against furniture on both sides, he closed his eyes and breathed. In and out, 1,2,3, a desperate attempt to connect to something peaceful. Meditation didn't come easy to him— nothing did, to be honest. Other people could relax into poses for minutes, hours... Todd could only manage sixty seconds on a good day. Instead of shutting off his brain, he found the practice offered clarity to the hellscape of disquieting thoughts in his head. It made his phobias pop with vibrancy, his innermost fears rattle around unrestrained. There was nothing spiritual about the experience. It was about as close to Hell as he could imagine, but he continued in an attempt to improve his mindset.

"Tea's here you twat!" his Gran called from outside the room.

Meditation wasn't going to happen.

Todd got up and walked to the kitchen, grabbing his tea. The mug was covered in British flags and pixellated pictures of the Queen. The entire house was a shrine to the monarchy, plastered in photos and displays of limited-edition memorabilia. There was barely anything he could touch that didn't have their faces or names on it.

He sipped his drink whilst pouring a bowl of cereal.

"You have to be on your best behaviour this afternoon, for Benjamin," Todd ordered.

"When do I ever misbehave? I'm seventy-three years old!" his Gran responded.

"That just means you've had that much more practice."

"Yeah, well tell you what: you're less than half my age, and you're already a rude little bugger."

Todd smirked, wolfing down the cereal whilst slumped against the kitchen counter.

"I learned from the best," he said, placing the bowl in the sink.

The lukewarm dishwater turned murky, remnants of milk diluting the liquid. Todd quickly ran a sponge over the inside of the bowl and placed it on the rack.

"Real-talk though, don't be telling him any of your dirty stories. He might pop his clogs. Have a cardiac incident."

His Gran slapped him on the arm, rolling her eyes.

"I'll tell him all the stories I want, thank you. If he wants to hear the dirty ones, then that's up to him. See if he can handle a woman like me…"

Todd gagged, pretending to vomit.

"It's not sealed up down there you know. I'm still a beautiful woman!"

The vomiting almost became a reality after that declaration.

"Right, bye! I'm going to my room," Todd started. He picked out a giant bag of popcorn, a two-litre bottle of coke, and a clean glass from the still-ajar cupboard, and shuffled towards his door.

"I'll tell Benjamin not to be too loud if we make it to the bedroom," his Gran cackled.

The poor man had no idea what he was walking into.

CHAPTER 7

MAGGIE

The road into Egglemore was packed full of vehicles, a slow-moving conga line of frustrated passengers rolling into town. There was no way Maggie was going to miss this appointment. Wedged between a HGV and some kind of tiny electric car, Maggie had limited options. She could try and pull into the other lane, see if it moved at a slightly quicker pace than this one. But it would be a marginal victory at best, most likely gaining nothing at all.

Instead, she flicked on the indicator and pulled left, ramming an orange roadworks cone out of the way. With total disregard for the law (the stress of getting another appointment was worth the consequences), Maggie sped down the lane, blaring her horn to alert the road workers. Frightened men in neon orange jumped out of her path, screaming profanities only audible for a moment. They drifted away in the rearview whilst Maggie kept her eyes set firmly on the end of the lane.

A wall of metal was speeding towards her, road signs and some kind of crane forming a barricade. She had to time her exit just right, to ensure a few cones would be the only casualties of her joyride. Gently applying the brake, Maggie swerved through the boundary line, crunching over a dusty mix of cement and broken brick.

"This isn't safe, Mum!" Claire moaned.

"I know it's not. Quiet."

A blur of signs. Warnings. Workers. Tools.

At the last second, Maggie forced the steering wheel to the right and hurtled into the slow lane. She quickly applied the brake to avoid rear-ending the car in front of her, and then the vehicle settled. She exhaled, feeling a wash of relief.

Claire's mouth was agape. Maggie ignored her, silently lamenting the selective times her hearing decided to kick in. The road in front of them was clear now, a direct route to the hospital. The quicker they got there, the quicker they could get out, ideally without any commitment to return to the city for a long time.

Maggie coasted into a small parking space, the only one available in the modest lot. The hospital was made up of a sprawling network of interconnected grey buildings, imposing multi-storey structures completely devoid of personality. A steady stream of visitors flowed through the entrance, with several more spotted around the smoking area and taxi bays.

"Get your speedy legs on," Maggie said, rushing ahead of her daughter. Claire trailed behind, engrossed in a video on her phone.

The reception desk sat at the far side of a large, triple-storey entrance, which branched off into different hallways and waiting areas. Behind the desk, a huge information board detailed the various wards and departments, which Maggie scanned with unwavering focus.

"Okay. Level C, let's go."

Claire had hardly caught up before her mum was on the move again, stomping towards the lift area. The first elevator was packed full of people and a couple of wheelchairs, so they'd have to wait for another one. Impatiently, Maggie tapped the *call* button repeatedly, listening out for the familiar ding of a free lift.

Eventually, another one arrived, and Maggie pushed in front of the queue to secure her spot.

"Come on," she gestured to Claire, whose legs were already starting to ache. Claire followed suit, apologising as she shifted into position, her back against the metal interior. As the doors slid closed, a piercing scream reverberated through the shaft. The visitors shared a curious glance before returning to their awkward silence.

The endless maze of corridors and dead ends were a notable feature of this "mega hospital", who had to hire staff just to direct patients to the correct departments. It was the latest in a long line of cost-saving measures, having absorbed a few smaller hospitals and service providers. A few years ago, Maggie would have been able to get an appointment at her local GP rather than making the trek to Egglemore, but it wasn't an option anymore. Instead, she was inside this monotonous behemoth of a building, trying her best not to recall any of the awful memories tied to it.

Eventually, the sign for *audiology* came into view, leading to one more corridor and a smaller waiting area. Maggie marched up to the desk and Claire took a seat.

"Hello. Margaret Bunton, here for my daughter, Claire."

"Just a moment," the receptionist said, tapping on the keyboard.

Maggie pushed down the lever on a hand sanitiser station and rubbed her hands with the clear liquid.

"It says here you had an appointment last month, is that right?"

Maggie's eye twitched.

"That isn't right, no. We've been rescheduled a number of times."

"Riiiight," the young woman behind the desk said, drawing out the word as she gazed at the monitor.

Maggie checked over her shoulder quickly. Claire was back on her phone, texting and laughing at something.

"Oh here we are. So you'll be seeing Dr. Jacobs, but unfortunately he is running a bit behind."

"How far behind?" Maggie questioned.

"There's a screen on the wall over there with current waiting times."

Maggie followed the woman's gaze and read the text on-screen.

We are currently running an average of 120mins behind planned appointment times. We apologise for any inconvenience.

"Two hours? Is there no-one else we can see?"

The woman shook her head apologetically.

"I'm sorry for the inconvenience. There's a café on Level B if you'd like some lunch whilst you wait."

Maggie sighed, slinking away from the desk. The dull, sanitised furnishings in the room were as uninspiring as they come, and she couldn't bear sitting in one place for so long. And don't get her started on the "reading material" available to peruse in the room. It was only ever *Landscaping Monthly* or some celebrity gossip rag, and neither of those things held her interest. With a background in IT and security, Maggie's brain preferred coding over chrysanthemums.

Maggie tapped Claire on the shoulder.

"Right. We have to wait, so let's get some lunch."

Claire finished typing a message and looked up at her mum.

"What do they have?"

"A café," Maggie complained. "Might get a panini, if we're lucky."

Claire chuckled and stood back up, shaking her legs to stop them aching so much.

"Can we take a slower walk there? My thighs are jelly from trying to keep up."

"Whatever you need, slow coach."

CHAPTER 8

ALICE

Blonde Hair's face was lacerated with deep cuts, his neck angled awkwardly towards the sky. Just in front of the stalled vehicle, he was crumpled over the concrete boundary, torn clothes hanging limp on his frame.

Alice only caught a glimpse of him, but it was enough.

"We need to call someone," she said, to no-one in particular, before noticing the boy's friend over the way. His face was red with tears, swollen bruises marring the topography of his handsome face. As she started towards him, Alice noticed an ambulance sitting idly just by the entrance to the services. A male paramedic, around her age or just older, was sprinting over towards them, clutching his medical pack.

"Over here!" Alice called, forcing her way to the front of the crowd. The paramedic arrived and immediately got to work, hands rifling through the pack. A second paramedic rushed out of the building, on his way to join his partner.

"What happened?" the first paramedic asked, scouting the area.

"He wouldn't stop," Brown Hair whispered, his voice barely audible.

"There was a big fight and then this idiot crashed into the wall! I'm meant to be watching football in two hours!"

Alice glared in the direction of her neighbouring passenger, shutting him up before he could continue. The driver of the coach was nowhere to be seen, having fled inside to throw up.

"We crashed after the tyre popped," Alice interjected. "The guy on the floor was attacking—"

"Jake," Brown Hair piped up. "His name is Jake."

Alice questioned his use of the present tense. The way that boy's head was angled, there was no coming back from that. It was a shock response, probably. Or some kind of misguided hope.

"Did you call the police already?" the paramedic asked.

Alice shook her head. Someone in the crowd mumbled that they'd take care of it.

"And what's your name?" the paramedic asked Brown Hair, intermittently talking into his radio.

"Rhys," he said.

"Rhys, I need you to step back over there. And the rest of you, let us do our job."

"Is he okay?" Rhys asked.

The paramedic paused. His partner slowed to a jog and headed straight over to Blonde Hair.

"We need to check for a pulse," the paramedic answered. "Please."

He gestured towards Alice, and her journalistic instinct kicked in.

"Rhys? Let's get a coffee, shall we?"

The pair started towards the service station. Rhys looked over his shoulder until they were far from the scene, and then just stared down at his feet.

The interior was a circus of bright fast food signs and vibrant, yet obviously worn, furniture. Alice had no idea where they were. There were only three main stops on the motorway, and they were still too far out for it to be Egglemore Interchange.

The answer was written in garish *comic sans* type on a massive sign: "Timeout Central". The building was huge, broken up by dividers and vendors and a rabble of directionless visitors with no sense of urgency. They were daydreaming about their holidays or journeys or what syrup to get in their mochas, completely oblivious to the gorefest outside.

"I don't actually drink coffee," Rhys declared.

"That's okay. They'll have soft drinks," Alice answered. The boy was obviously in shock, and despite a genuine feeling of empathy, she also knew that it would be a perfect time to get a statement from him. Something was unfolding, and it could make a great story. Especially with all the emotions and feelings so fresh in her subject's mind.

He'd just seen his friend die in front of him, in the most brutal and intimate way possible. And he was *technically* partly to blame for the accident that led to his demise. That was juicy. That was *raw*.

"Can we get one for Jake too? For when he wakes up?" Rhys said.

Alice felt uneasy guilt brewing in her stomach. But she had to focus. She had a job to do, after all.

"Sure. Does he drink coffee?"

Rhys nodded. "Caramel extra shot. Extra hot. He's the fussy brother."

Alice stopped.

"Brother?"

Rhys looked at her, the first eye contact since they'd left the group.

"Yeah, Jake. He's my brother."

"Oh, I'm sorry. I thought he was your friend."

Rhys nodded.

"He *is* sometimes. Other times, well. A pain in the ass."

Alice smiled at that.

They settled on a table in the back corner of the main seating area, taking over a tray with coffees and pastries, plus a cloudy lemonade for Rhys. Alice grabbed her phone and placed it on the table, face down of course. The voice recorder app was already open, creating a digital copy of their entire conversation. It wasn't completely by the book, but sometimes you had to act first and ask for forgiveness later.

"Where are you headed?" Alice asked, questions rolling before they were even in their seats.

"Home," he sighed.

"Not a fan of Egglemore?"

"It's not that. We're due to compete."

Alice raised an eyebrow.

"Gymnastics. We've been training *hard*. Our family is gonna be there."

"There'll be other times," Alice said, trying to sound reassuring. Rhys didn't look so sure.

The rest of the conversation was just as stimulating. He wasn't making much sense.

"We better get back out. This will go cold," he said, gesturing to the coffee. His eyes were blank, devoid of any warmth, as if reality was slowly sinking in.

"Can I ask you a question?" Alice asked.

He nodded, barely moving his head.

"How was Jake this morning? Were there any signs he was unwell?"

"What do you mean? He wasn't unwell."

"Just in terms of his behaviour. I saw him acting erratically before the… scuffle."

Rhys looked into her eyes. It might as well have been her soul.

"There was nothing wrong. I'd know if there was. He got up early, had a nap on the coach, then…"

"Then?" Alice angled forward, closing the gap between them.

"He was crying. His face was… twisted, like…"

Tears pooled in his eyes, reflecting the strip lights above. "I need to get back to him. Give him this before it gets cold."

Rhys grabbed the drinks and jogged back to the entrance, disappearing out the door. Alice stretched her neck, shaking off the dull ache the collision had brought on earlier. She'd make a note of any symptoms, just in case. She didn't like to file insurance claims, but if the injury had any effect on her ability to work, she'd have to explore her options.

"What the fuck is he doing?"

A scream roared from across the building. Seconds later, a dozen people joined in.

Alice switched to her camera app, and rushed over to the chicken fast food vendor across the way, filming everything she could. Through a crowd of petrified faces, Alice saw a teenage boy flopped behind the counter, his right arm sizzling in a deep fat fryer. His piercing shriek joined the chorus of chaos, intermittently distorting into a guttural bark.

"Someone pull him down!" Alice screamed, a jolt of excitement hidden under her concerned exterior.

One person was a coincidence. Two is the start of something huge.

The boy slipped to the floor, splashing a pool of oil from the fryer onto his face. His features dissolved, melting into a milky-tan soup of hair and flesh. Flailing, he forced himself back to his feet.

He inhaled deeply.

Froze in his place.

Cautiously, he lifted his hands in front of his face, transfixed by the sizzling blisters eating away at his skin.

Hands down.

Head up.

The boy snarled—and broke into a sprint.

"Somebody stop him!"

Alice couldn't see who those words belonged to. She was too focused on filming the kid.

Breaking through a pair of onlookers, the boy charged across the dining hall, right into a thick concrete pillar. His body cracked and fell limply to the floor. Alice watched the whole thing through her phone, instinctively jolting when he made impact.

Her mouth hung wide open in disbelief at the scene unfolding before her. A voice stuttered from somewhere near the entrance.

"Have you seen my boy?"

A rugged looking man, early 40s, plaid top and denim jeans. Bodybuilder-shaped. His eyes scanned the space frantically, falling upon the crumpled mess on the floor. Alice captured every second.

"Oh my God!" he screamed, running over to his burnt, unconscious child, trying to wake him. His bear-like hands wrapped around the boy's shoulders, shaking his jellied face into a new pattern. Alice zoomed in on the man's face, capturing his horrified squeal.

The networks would love this footage.

A reflection through the window—the paramedic from earlier.

He was sprinting back towards his vehicle, panic painted across his face. Alice turned to look, and in a distorted blur, he slammed down into the pavement, a female stranger bashing his face in with two heavy fists. The rest of the coach group were barely visible in the distance, piling back onto the vehicle.

The rugged man in plaid jumped up from beside his son and made a beeline for the front door, sprinting straight towards this deranged woman. Did he know her?

The paramedic's head was a crushed watermelon, and now...

What was she doing?

Alice tiptoed towards the window, as if making a sound could make the situation worse. As she approached, the grotesque sight outside became even clearer.

The woman thrust her face into the paramedic's gaping cavity, viscous red staining her mouth and cheeks. With an aggressive tug and snatch, she whipped her head left to right, guzzling remnants of flesh with deep gulps.

Alice felt light, invisible even. Out of body, just like a dream. There was no way in Hell this was real. Maybe she'd fallen asleep on the coach.

"KERRY, STOP!"

The man was outside now. Reaching out for the woman. His wife, perhaps?

"Cack, deerrgg hell!" She was trying to speak, spitting syllables in place of words. Then they were gone, thrust out of view in a violent clash. Alice followed the action, filming from the safety of the inside. They were both on the floor, then standing.

The woman snapped her teeth together, like a rabid dog.

The man was armed with a wrench. God only knew where he got it. Alice's brain was filling in the gaps, supporting her subconscious whilst it caught up with reality.

CLUNK.

The metal connected with her skull in one fell swoop, carving out a lump of skin and gristle. With outstretched arms, the woman shoved the man, causing them both to tumble over a low metal fence. Frenzied hands pulled, scratched, and slapped, a storm of violence.

Alice was losing sight of them. She couldn't afford to do that.

With her personal safety a distant memory, she side-stepped across to the entrance. Adrenaline pulsed through her body whilst she decided whether to open the door or just retreat back to the food hall.

Focus.

Alice slipped through the entrance, her phone trained on the warring couple. Small pockets of onlookers were staring in utter shock, unintentional bystanders to this battle. Alice kept the pair in her sights, recording everything blow-by-blow. Part of her thought she should intervene. Then she remembered the wildlife documentaries she used to adore as a child, and the cameramen who were only allowed to watch as the animals tore each other to shreds, bound by ethics to let nature run its course.

Plus, if she got involved, who was going to record this footage? Her role was to watch, document, and distribute. The audience was dissipating now, suddenly aware that this was no everyday fistfight. In the background, barely visible in the silhouetted courtyard outside the building, Rhys was stumbling around with his head in the clouds, cold coffee still in his hands.

He must have realised there was no saving his brother.

What was left of him, anyway...

His eyes were locked in a confused stare, body completely oblivious to the environment. Alice couldn't intervene. She just couldn't.

"Rhys! Over here!"

The words spilled from her mouth, some kind of subconscious self-sabotage for allowing herself to get into this position. To her surprise, Rhys clocked her and started around the small patch of grass in front. Unfortunately, her outburst caught the attention of Kerry, the crazy stranger, too.

The bloodthirsty woman snapped backwards, her head unnaturally angled in Alice's direction. The rest of her body followed suit. She was gaining on her, red-stained lips drawn back like a Rottweiler, arms wide and ready to pounce.

The woman filled the frame of Alice's camera, phone still locked on the action—but she didn't make contact.

Instead, the rugged survivor grabbed his wife mid-air and

slammed her down onto the concrete. With her head in the road and body splayed on the footpath, he pummelled the woman in the back of the head, opening up a wet cavern in her skull. Sloshy brain matter oozed out of the splintered crack. Another strike finished the job.

The man vomited up everything in his stomach. Alice felt like she could do the same.

She ended the recording.

CHAPTER 9

CHARLES

Every meal was a blessing. But when it came from *Rod's Subs*, it was transcendent. Belly full and energy levels right back up there, Charles said goodbye to his friend, and left with an invite to come back at any time.

After another half hour or so, Charles was at a grungy underpass on the north side of town. He'd kept his tent there for a couple of weeks, and it had worked out so far. His "neighbours" were respectable and kept to themselves, and though there was plenty of drug and alcohol use, they knew not to get him involved.

That said, Charles would never let himself get too attached to one place in particular—it was inevitable he'd be moved on in due course. The best thing to do was enjoy the present moment, and work out the rest as it came. *That's a life motto if ever there was one.*

"Hey J," he said, waving to an older man in an adjacent tent. "How's Janine?"

The man nodded, and gestured a thumbs up. "Asleep. It's peaceful for once."

Charles cracked a smile. Eventually, the older man did too.

"Surprised to see you in the day," he called over.

"Just gotta grab a new pencil and some water. I'm thirsty as Hell out here."

The man grunted and returned inside his tent, worn mesh panels providing much less privacy than designed. Charles unzipped his tunnel tent, forcing the zip all the way open. The fabric was frayed and kept catching in the mechanism, but until something better came around, he wasn't in a place to get rid of it.

Inside, dark blue walls cascaded down to an off-white floor. As much as it was a tight fit, Charles had plenty of basics to hand: water, snacks, wet wipes, medicine, miscellaneous electronics (and dozens of batteries to give them power). He grabbed a small travel bag and popped a few pills from worn blister packaging. With a swig of water, he gulped them down, wincing at the bitter aftertaste. After sitting for a few moments, he rifled through a case and grabbed a few fresh pencils, decanting them into his messenger bag. The water bottle followed, and he was on the move again.

On his way out, he heard a weird, muffled sound from his friend's tent. A gargled speech of some kind. He hoped Janine wasn't falling back into the substance issues. She was a lovely lady with a great smile and a big brain. She deserved so much better.

With the nostalgic sound of the turn of the century back in his ears, Charles revisited his notebook, eager to cross another name off of his list before sunset. He didn't have many leads at the moment, so would have to enter a research phase of sorts.

He'd had a fair share of luck around this area of the city, so it was a perfect time to scout out any of his previous guardian angels. There was a woman who worked at the drugstore, who'd once given him ten pounds to get some supplies. A man who lived around the corner had brought him leftovers in the rain, and he was pretty sure he knew where to find him.

Charles' trail of thought was broken by a sudden convoy of black cars, a handful of unmarked vehicles racing through a residential street. One of them pulled over into a driveway; the others continued their journey. A man in a business suit jumped out of the passenger side and trotted over to one of the houses.

Intrigued, Charles replaced his notebook and stalked behind a bush, trying to get a good vantage point. He could see a woman at the door, holding a young baby. The conversation seemed serious. The woman disappeared, but didn't shut the door. Was she getting something?

Charles shuffled, bending a few branches back to get a clear sight. Within mere moments, the woman returned in a coat, wielding a suitcase in one hand and a baby carrier in the other. She slipped in the back and the car sped off.

It was a strange sight, no doubt. He gulped another mouthful of water and started back on his route.

Halfway down a random alley near the centre of town, Charles bent over and spewed his lunch over a pile of black bin bags, wiping his mouth with the sleeve of his jacket. He really ought to have had his tablets with food, but kept forgetting to pack them in his bag. Now they were swimming in the beige mouth stew, and he'd probably have to take a double dose later.

A local community project, *Back On Your Feet,* was based out of a community centre on the high street and offered access to GPs and all sorts of help with paperwork and legal matters. He'd first discovered them by accident almost a decade ago, searching for a safe place to stay when he was evicted from a rental property. Since then, he'd attended every two weeks like clockwork, taking advantage of the services he could get.

Charles pushed open the door into the building, and settled on a chair in a small waiting room. He grabbed a ticket and started a new drawing whilst waiting for his number to be called, and when his turn came up, he greeted the doctor with a warm smile.

"Your bloods are more promising this week. Have you been having any side effects?"

Charles shook his head. The doctor didn't seem so sure.

"I know I ask the same thing every week, but have you reconsidered what we spoke about yet?"

Charles smiled politely, and shook his head again. The doctor stared at him sympathetically, clicking her pen rhythmically whilst she formulated a response.

"Okay. I'll order some more pills for next time you're here."

"Thank you," Charles said. "Now that's out of the way, how was Tenerife?"

The doctor smiled, and reeled off details of a late summer getaway, painting a picture that Charles couldn't help but get lost in.

CHAPTER 10
TODD

"Okay, perfume?" Todd asked.

"Check," his Grandma answered.

"Dinner prepped?"

"Check."

"Clean underwear?"

Todd's Gran rolled her eyes. A knock at the door saved them both from the discomfort of whatever might come next.

"Okay, he's here. Off to your room."

"Geez, someone's keen," Todd joked. "I can hear through my door, don't forget."

It was barely 3:00pm, but his Gran loved an early dinner, and if Benjamin wanted anything to do with her, he'd have to get used to it too.

She waved him away, and Todd took her direction. He flashed her a cheeky look from behind the door and closed it.

A freeze-frame of a beautiful French woman lingered on his monitor screen. Backdropped by a palatial garden, the image was a beautiful composition, just like a lot of cinema from that period. Todd adored foreign cinema, and had a notebook full of real locations from films and plans to visit every single one. France. Spain. Italy. The list was endless, and ambitious beyond belief.

Todd had never been on a plane, let alone roamed the gardens of stately homes or swanned around an exotic beach. The mere thought of the logistics involved in international travel kept Todd firmly rooted in Egglemore. The way his brain worked, it would take separate day trips with rest days between just to complete the journey, and that included the initial train to the airport.

One day, though. One day, he'd tick off every place and have a brain full of special memories and a heart full of joy. Until then, he lived vicariously through piles of vintage DVDs and old films on the internet.

When the film was finished, along with most of the snacks Todd had in the room, he decided to take the drone back out for a spin. A couple of his clients had cancelled, so it was a rare chance to check out the streets in the afternoon, rather than the early hours.

He started on the estate grounds, coasting around the apartment buildings. Families sat in the lounge, sharing stories about their days. One man was working out in his kitchen, dressed only in a pair of white boxer shorts, obviously open to the idea of being watched by the residents. Otherwise, it was a lineup of smokers out on the balcony, people watching TV, and one or two gossiping elderly people. Curiously, on the fourth floor of the building next to Todd's, a girl was holding a notepad up to her bedroom window. He'd never seen her before—the building wasn't entirely visible from Todd's flat. There was no way of knowing any finer details about the girl from this distance, she was just a blurry silhouette.

Todd pushed the control lever forwards, trying to pull off a gentle approach. Instead, his hand slipped, sending the aircraft directly into the window. He couldn't hear the sound of it slamming into the glass, but the girl definitely did. She jumped back, nearly dropping her notepad.

"Shit, shit, shit," Todd muttered, pulling back as calmly as he could. The drone behaved this time, drifting back in a steady pattern. The girl threw up her hands, silently gesturing *what the fuck.*

"Sorry, oh God," he sighed, as if she could hear him.

She shook with what looked like a belly laugh, raising her middle finger to the drone. Then, she put the notepad back up to the window.

Determined not to fuck up a second time, Todd nailed the approach, finally able to read the text on the page.

"Stop watching me, perv."

Oh God damn.

Todd laughed, then fell silent in an effort to decipher the intent of that message. Was she being serious? Or was her previous joking a sign of her just messing about?

Plus, that message was already written. Had she seen his drone before?

In a panic, Todd recalled the aircraft, quickly snatching it back through the window when it returned. He hoped that she didn't know where he lived. That would be so fucking awkward. In fact, it was probably better never to see her again. He'd make every effort to avoid that floor.

On the other hand… Todd was bored out of his mind, and it felt like the right day to try something different. Hell, his Nan had a man over, if ever there was a day for ballsy, uncharacteristic moves, it was today.

He might fall on his face, and be labelled as a weird voyeur for the rest of his days. But he might just make a new friend, someone to force him out of his box and experience the real world a little bit.

Fuck it.

Todd tore a sheet from a notepad and grabbed a sharpie.

He scribbled *"Chat?"* in big letters on both sides, followed by his phone number. It was the bravest thing he'd done in years. Overthinking would take over his brain if he waited too long, so he fastened the note to the drone arm with a shoelace and an unhealthy amount of sticky tape. If the wind caught it, he'd written his information on both sides. If he didn't get a call or a text message, he'd take the hint and leave her alone.

"Okay Toddy. You got this," he muttered to himself. He rested the drone on this windowsill and flew it up to the top of the buildings. Carefully navigating the treetops, he twisted the vehicle around a few obstacles and landed on the girl's balcony. It hovered, barely balancing on the railing. Todd couldn't tell if the note was still attached, but he'd get a hint when she looked out the window.

A fraction of a second later, she appeared. Her face beamed with a youthful glow, curious eyebrows framing her forehead. Smiling, she grabbed a phone from her pocket and started typing.

Oh shit, oh shit.

Safe to say the note was still attached. Safe to say Todd was shitting a brick.

Like clockwork, his phone buzzed. The drone was slipping, so he couldn't read it yet. Coasting back the way it came, Todd willed it to speed up, pacing back and forth until it finally recalled. He didn't waste any time dragging it back into his room and discarding it on the floor.

Hi. I'm Tanya.

Todd's fingers hovered over the screen for a moment, before he typed out a reply.

Hey. I'm Todd. 25 years old.

Why are you telling me your age?

> I don't know. Icebreaker?

Okay. I'm 31. Do you know what's going on at 542?

> No. I can't see it from here.

Okay, it's right above me. You should fly your camera plane thing up there. And tell me what's happening. I can hear someone smashing up their house or something.

> Why don't you go up there?

I don't know them. That would be weird.

It couldn't be any weirder than spying on them with a camera, but why not?

> Okay. The flat above yours?

She replied with a thumbs up. Todd couldn't help but associate that emoji with sarcasm or passive aggressive behaviour. He preferred a love heart reaction to his messages, it felt warmer, but she wouldn't know that yet.

The drone's battery light was flashing intermittently. It needed charging. It always needed charging.

Todd grabbed the plug and connected the USB to the chassis. The light flickered from red to yellow, signalling the start of its charge.

> I have to charge my drone for a bit. I'll check it out though.

Okay. Report back. And no peeking through my curtains tonight please.

What? I don't do that.

I'm joking idiot. Report back tho for sure x

Now Todd was replaying all of his journeys back, wondering if he'd ever strayed past the girl's window accidentally. He'd only filmed at night three times. It was very unlikely. He decided to park that thought for now.

Will do.

She didn't reply after that, but Todd checked his phone a dozen or so times to make sure.

Halfway through an Italian Giallo from the '80s, his phone buzzed again.

Now there's just screaming. I think the husband is alone, but there could be people in there. How long until we take off and check this shit out?

Todd chuckled. It would only be a short journey. He could fly half-charged.

Okay I'm impatient too. I'll check it now.

She responded with a love-heart reaction to his message. Moments later, the drone was mid-air, the ratty note still attached. On the approach to apartment 542, Todd could immediately tell something was wrong. Furniture was strewn across the living room, as if someone had purposefully trashed the house. There were dark stains splattered on the windows. The glass was cracked, splintered shards poking from the frame. A silhouette stalked through the rooms in the background, contorted and frantic.

Todd wanted to tell the girl, try and explain what he was seeing.

The silhouette paced into the light and slammed into the front window. Todd could make out the face now. A man, mid 50s maybe. Business suit. Blood spread through his beard. Bloodshot eyes locked on the drone.

"Oh shit."

Moments later, the man was out on the balcony, lunging at the aircraft. Todd panicked, pulling away sharply. Somehow, the drone lurched forwards, and the crazed suit brushed it with his fingertips. Unfazed, he tried again, slicing his hand in the process. Blood trickled over the drone camera, creating a muddy brown image.

The recall button wasn't working. Todd flicked the switch a half dozen times, but the machine didn't react. The autopilot function was still available, thank God, so he toggled that on momentarily.

Shit.

He checked that the drone was maintaining its position, then threw the controls onto his chair. As it was, the man could knock the aircraft out of the sky with another lunge, so time was of the essence.

Todd grabbed his phone.

> Something's wrong with 542. We need to call the police.

> What? I'm not a snitch

> No. You don't understand. He's gone crazy.

A few seconds passed before the next reply.

> Crazy? Maybe we should keep out of it then.

Out of it? She'd been the one to suggest spying on the

man, and now she was having second thoughts? He was a danger to himself, out there flailing by the balcony railing.

> He's going to fall if he's not careful. We need to...

Todd stopped typing, alerted to the controls by a piercing, tinny alarm. It was built into the device, usually sounding when the drone was heading towards a collision or out of bounds.

On-screen, more blood was spread across the lens, and a smattering of lacerations were painted across the business-man's face. He was the picture of rage, smashing the air around him in an attempt to connect with the aircraft. Todd hit the *recall* button, desperately praying it would work this time.

And it did, slowly sliding away from the chaos. Todd's phone buzzed in his pocket.

Okay. Steady. Steady.

The man wailed, mouth twisted into an unnatural shape, eyes hollow with despair. After a slight stumble backwards, he stormed towards the edge of the balcony, thrusting his hands at the buzzing whir of the blades. His hip cracked against the railing, doubling him over the sketchy metal structure. Via the camera, Todd saw the man's feet lift from the ground. He stayed trapped on the railing, his weight somehow counterbalanced. His limbs thrashed, trying to force his frame one way or the other, but it was no use. It would have been comedic if it wasn't so damn dangerous.

Was he drunk? On drugs? Both?

Todd kept the autopilot mode engaged and called 999. He ran through the questions at lightning speed, and could hear sirens within a matter of minutes. A red fire engine tore through the one-way street leading into the vicinity, and two firefighters rapidly erected a ladder from the truck up to the fifth-floor balcony. A couple of police cars arrived moments later.

It was a wave of action, the most the estate had seen in a few weeks. Things had been strangely quiet recently, a sense of foreboding perhaps. One firefighter was already scaling the ladder whilst the other relayed information to the police escort.

"Todd? Is something going on out there?" his Gran called.

"Someone's on the balcony. Firefighters are here."

He heard the screech of the chair legs and a pitter patter to the door. His Gran was a one-woman neighbourhood watch and she couldn't let any gossip pass her by. Another shuffling sound suggested Benjamin might share the pastime.

"I can't see nothing," she called through the door. Todd opened it up, and joined the lovebirds at the window.

"Fifth floor, I think. We can't see from here."

His Gran snatched her dressing gown from a hook by the door and quickly dragged Benjamin out to get a better look. Todd turned to go back into his room, but was caught by another question.

"How do you know it's on the fifth floor?"

Todd stopped in his tracks, trying to formulate a response. He didn't want to admit he was antagonising the residents with his drone.

"Saw something on Facebook," he called out, then went to hide in his room.

The drone was hovering above the window ledge outside, and he quickly brought it back in, hoping none of his nosy neighbours had seen what happened. From the corner of his eye, he could see some kind of scuffle on the ladder. The truth was, he had a perfect view from his room, right up to the balcony. But he didn't want his Gran hanging around all night. Or Benjamin, as lovely as he was.

The angry businessman was frantically squirming, his feet back on the balcony now. The firefighter fought to restrain him, but it wasn't working. He was teetering on the ladder rung, trying to calm him down.

In a swift movement, the businessman yanked the fire-fighter's helmet from his head, and launched it down towards the street. Seconds later, he was pulling him by the hair, trying to tell him something. No. It was more than that.

It was feral. The man had completely lost it.

He was trying to *bite* him.

"Gran?"

She was there in moments, pulling Benjamin along with her.

"You can see it all from here! Why did you make us go out in the cold?"

She didn't make eye contact with Todd once. Her eyes were transfixed by the conflict.

Todd's phone buzzed. Repeatedly.

"Oh my God," he whispered, as the man tore a chunk right out of the firefighter's neck, causing an eruption of blood to rain down like a fountain. The rusty crimson glittered as it gushed down the ladders.

The fireman's grip on the ladders relaxed, and he leant backwards, free-falling past each of the floors. His limp body contorted in the air before careening straight into the ladder mount on the truck roof. The metal frame imploded on impact, shattering the windows and windscreen.

A chorus of screams echoed through the courtyard. When reality set in, Todd found himself joining them.

CHAPTER 11

MAGGIE

The café was as uninspiring as Maggie had expected. She and Claire wolfed down a room-temperature cheese sandwich and some stale crisps before slowly walking back to the waiting area.

Maggie hated waiting. It was something ingrained in her since a child, the idea of wasting time just sitting or idling. She preferred to run to a schedule, get shit done, and then get out.

Especially somewhere like Egglemore, with the world's worst traffic and passive aggressive residents always ready to stop for an argument. That might have been a biased view, but it's the one she held.

Finally, the receptionist called Claire's name, and Maggie marched up to the small treatment room with her.

"Claire Bunton. I'm her mum, Maggie."

The doctor nodded, cross referencing her notes.

"Come in."

Maggie took a seat by the door, letting Claire and the doctor discuss the issue.

"Right, Claire. I've looked at your notes and some of the

treatments you've had before. How would you say your hearing is right now?"

Almost comically, Claire leaned in, adjusting the angle of her ear more towards the doctor.

"I guess that gives you an answer," Claire joked. Maggie chuckled too.

"I'm going to take a look at your ears in a moment, but I wanted to discuss my one thing first. Have you heard of SSHL at all?"

Claire looked to her mum, shaking her head. Maggie mirrored the gesture.

"It means Sudden Sensorineural Hearing Loss. It affects around six thousand people a year, and encompasses a few of your symptoms. Usually, it affects those in their forties or fifties, and often resolves sporadically. But you have some symptoms that don't line up with this, so we'll have to do some more tests before confirming."

Claire nodded, concern darkening her face.

"Will the hearing come back?" Maggie asked, dragging her chair closer to the doctor and her daughter.

"It often resolves spontaneously. To be completely honest, in medical terms there is a lot we don't understand about the condition. But there are options for treatment and plenty of things to try, so I wouldn't be too worried."

Maggie nodded. She was already worried. Her daughter looked so small and fragile in the seat. Maggie wished she could do something to help.

"I'm going to check your ears now and we'll do a few tests." She turned to Maggie. "Does mum want to stay or wait outside?"

Claire cleared her throat.

"Can you stay, Mum?"

"Of course I can."

The doctor shuffled a few papers and grabbed a clipboard.

"I'm going to order an MRI and some bloods. I just need

to run this down the hall, as the IT system is glitching. Apologies for the inconvenience."

"How long should these tests take?" Maggie asked, respectfully. "Only so I know whether to extend my car parking."

The doctor looked a little flustered.

"We're running very behind, I won't sugar coat it, Ms Bunton. Ideally we should have them all done within a couple of hours."

Maggie nodded, deflated. More waiting.

The entrance to the hospital was a hive of activity. Maggie walked back through the rotating doors and into the car park, pulling out her phone. Walking as she tapped her phone, she pulled up a contact name: *"David"*.

David was a demon amongst men, the worst of the worst. But he was also Claire's father, and when it came to anything medical or serious like that, she felt it right to share the news. Apprehensively, she hit the *call* button.

A few rings later, he answered with a groan.

"We didn't have a call booked in today. I'm seeing Claire next Sunday."

"Hello to you too, David. How are you?"

She smirked, knowing just how to get on his nerves.

"What is it, Margaret?"

"I'm at Egglemore Hospital. Claire's hearing has gotten worse."

"How much worse?" he answered, eventually sounding like he was actually paying attention.

"They're doing tests. I'll keep you updated, of course, but she's in good spirits."

"How long has the appointment been booked for? I should have been there."

Maggie sighed silently, knowing exactly how conversations with this man went. She looked both ways, crossed over the road, and headed to the pay machine.

"It's been rescheduled five times. It was last minute, otherwise I would have told you."

A few moments of silence.

"Well, I want to be at the next one. I'm on a business trip so I have to go, but please *text* me later if there's any issues. Please only call in an emergency, or at the set times I speak to Claire. Goodbye."

He hung up. Maggie rolled her eyes and grabbed some coins from her pocket, pushing them into the slot one by one. After paying for a few more hours, she turned and caught a glimpse of something strange in one of the cars. The windows were fogged up, not a surprise in this weather, but someone seemed to be locked in the front seat. Cautiously, she stalked around to the front of the car, and tried to look closer without appearing nosy.

It was an elderly woman with thinning grey hair and deep wrinkles etched into her skin. Her face was solemn, mouth hung open and dripping with sticky saliva. Ordinarily, Maggie didn't like to get involved in other people's business, but something about her mannerisms didn't sit right.

Sporadically, the woman arched forwards, clawing at the dashboard in front of her. It was as if she was trying to pull herself up and through the windscreen, but in a frantic, frankly deranged way.

Perhaps she had dementia or a similar condition? Maggie didn't know nearly enough about medical things to make a determination, but she thought it best to check the woman was okay. She looked around to see if anyone was lingering near the pay machines, perhaps having just hopped out to pay for the car park. But no-one looked over, so Maggie was going to take it upon herself to be a good citizen.

"Excuse me, is everything okay?"

Maggie noticed the window was cracked open at the top, as though the old woman was a little dog left in the summer sun.

"Do you want me to open the door?" Maggie asked, trying to get some kind of reaction from the woman. "It's really no trouble if you want me to open it from this side."

The woman looked in Maggie's direction, but rather than making eye contact, she just looked straight through her. Maggie was stumped. She didn't know what to do.

"I'm going to see if there's anyone in reception who can help you," she said.

After a deep, lengthy inhale, the woman screamed at the top of her lungs, vocal cords unleashing a deep roar. She lunged forwards again, smacking brittle fists against the windscreen and window.

Maggie paced backwards, wary of appearing intimidating to the woman. She rushed away and into reception, then over to the sparse desk at the far corner.

"Hi, bit of a weird one. There's a lady out in the car park, she seems to be trapped in a car. I didn't want to open it without checking if there was a reason it's locked."

The receptionist looked as confused as Maggie felt.

"Okay, erm... I can get security to go and check it out." She looked over at a stocky security guard and waved him over.

"This lady said there is someone trapped in a car outside. Can you check it out?"

He nodded, and Maggie gave him some details to help direct him. With that, her good deed was done, and she continued onto the winding corridor that eventually led to the audiology department.

When she arrived, she was greeted by Claire, who was waiting on a chair.

"Where's the doctor?" Maggie asked. "Any news?"

"She got called to an emergency," Claire sighed. "Going to add some time to the tests, she thinks."

A storm brewed in Maggie's chest.

"I just went and extended the car park. Fuck sake."

Claire laughed.

"It's boring isn't it," she said, patting the chair next to her. "Let's watch cat videos whilst we wait."

Maggie did just that, chuckling at a frenzy of feline fails whilst she tried to keep some semblance of her patience. She'd give it ten minutes before complaining to the department receptionist.

"What sort of emergency do audiologists even have?" Maggie moaned, breaking out of the cat video trance. "Someone's ear fallen off or something?"

"Don't joke about that," Claire warned playfully. "That might be our next trip up here otherwise."

Maggie huffed.

"Yeah, let's not put that out into the universe."

CHAPTER 12
ALICE

Everyone outside the services had returned to the main building. A handful of bodies lay limp on the forecourt, blood and guts littering the tarmac.

The rugged man had lost his son (whose body had been dragged elsewhere) and had killed his own wife. Given the way the day had gone so far, Alice wondered what was going on with this place.

And where were the police?

Alice tapped some notes into her phone, trying to create a diary of the events so far. She got on the coach at 10:00am. By 12:00pm, they were at this service station and she'd already seen two corpses. That was more than she'd ever seen in her life, let alone in one day, and she felt ever so slightly troubled that she hadn't had more of a reaction to them.

It was now mid-afternoon.

"What you up to?" a man asked, plonking himself on the bench beside her. She was about to answer with a snarky comment before noticing her seat neighbour from the coach. His eyes were wide with fear, his voice more settled than usual.

"I'm just keeping track of the day," she answered simply. "Are you okay?"

"I mean, I've missed the football... But, that man... Did you see?"

Alice locked her phone and turned to him. He wasn't being as much of a prick as before. Maybe she'd scared him. And if he was suffering from shock, she might be able to get some kind of statement for her story. If he was antagonistic or rude, it would only generate stronger reactions to the piece she was writing, so she'd give him full creative license to be as much of a bastard as he fancied.

"Can I ask you a question?" Alice said. The man nodded.

"What do you think is causing all this?"

The man leant back on the bench, pondering.

"Well, *we're* not acting like it, are we?" he said, pointing out the obvious.

"I don't think so."

"Maybe they've been in contact with something?"

Alice scrunched her brow.

"I don't think so. That guy and his brother—"

"Brother?"

"Yep. They were fighting, so if it was physical contact—"

"He'd have it too," the man said, defeated.

"Exactly. So what else?"

The man shrugged.

"I don't know. I just want to leave. Has anyone seen the driver?"

Alice glanced over her shoulder, as if the driver might be right behind them, eavesdropping on the conversation.

"Someone said he got drunk and went to sleep in one of the motel rooms over the road."

"There's a motel here?"

"Sure is. That's where that family came from. The dad and the... well. Wife. Kid. You know... *Them.*" Alice gestured to the window, pointing out the wife's corpse.

"It doesn't make sense. I'm going to order a taxi or some-thing. I'll find the money, I just want to get out of here."

"Did anyone call the police earlier?" Alice asked, ignoring the man's whining.

He shrugged again, finding a new way to annoy her with every passing minute. Then he was gone, plodding over to the exit. Alice sighed and pulled out her phone, switching off the voice recorder app. No-one had told her anything remotely helpful yet. She'd have to find that boy, Rhys, again. Get him to say something interesting. She needed a good pull-quote.

"We called the police earlier. Three times."

Alice turned to see the elderly woman from the coach. Her husband was by her side, tending to his ruptured scalp and missing hair.

"On the coach earlier. He attacked you, right? The blonde boy?"

The elderly gentleman nodded, in pain but obviously enjoying being the centre of attention for once.

"We haven't been able to get him any medical attention," the wife interjected, before the man even had a chance to speak. "What happened to those paramedics?"

"One got attacked," Alice said. "About an hour ago. No idea where the other one went."

"Bloody typical. Well, what are we doing? We can't hang around here all day."

"I'm going to get a taxi. You're welcome to join me."

The woman nodded enthusiastically.

"That would be great. We're meeting our daughters for an event, and..."

Alice tuned out her voice, instead searching for a taxi app or a number for someone who'd pick her up from the side of a motorway. Eventually, she tracked down a company from the nearest town. They were willing to do the trip, but wouldn't be available for half an hour. Alice booked it, figuring it was probably the easiest way to the city before nightfall.

Just before she tucked her phone back in her pocket, a message popped up on-screen. It was from an encrypted messaging app she was using to correspond with her contact in Egglemore.

PRIVATE NUMBER

We need to meet soon if we're doing this.
Where are you now?

Alice exhaled, frustrated at the situation she found herself in.

ALICE

Still at the service station. Going to find a way to get to you.

PRIVATE NUMBER

Please hurry. We don't have much time.

CHAPTER 13

ROWAN

Everything was grey. What was the point of it anyway?

Ten years down the drain. A decade of beautiful memories, torn apart and burnt to a crisp.

And for what? A quick fling in a crusty hotel room with some slob from the office?

Rowan boiled the kettle and angrily went through the routine of making coffee for two. The same images had played on a loop in his head for the last couple of weeks ever since *she* told him about the affair. His beautiful wife, radiant auburn hair, delicate smile.

Now he could only imagine her on her back, legs open for some vile rat half her age. Rowan was slightly older than his wife, both in their early 40s. They both had successful careers and owned a beautiful home. No kids, though that had been her idea, not his. And here he was, making coffee for her as if things were normal.

As he stirred the gloopy granules into milky water, the torturous vision burned into his mind. He couldn't stop it.

Nor could he stop the heavy-handed preparation, smashing the spoon on the edge of the cup to remove any drips. The anger in his body manifested in violent twitches and bursts of frustration, usually at inanimate objects like the leaky milk bottle or creaky fridge door.

Rowan grabbed the tiny cup handles with his oversized, hairy hands, and walked out into the hallway.

Quickly setting aside the drinks to get the door, he twisted the doorknob and opened it outwards, revealing a dark abyss. After pulling a string light by the frame, he descended carefully into the basement.

"Honey. I made coffee. Should we chat?"

Rowan angled around a corner wall, and couldn't help but smile when he saw the woman he loved. Her soft waves were teased behind her ear, stray hairs plastered to her sweaty forehead. It reminded him of post-coital bliss, the scent of them both intermingled in the air, staring at each other's red-hued faces.

His wife snapped awake, her big eyes glossy with tears. Rowan had probably bound the restraints too tight; they must be uncomfortable. Her teeth were forced around a makeshift gag, dirty laundry shreds fashioned into a tight coil. Rowan placed the coffee down by her legs and untied the gag. His wife coughed, hacking up a frothy mixture of old saliva and blood.

Rowan took a seat on a dusty dining room chair, piled up alongside various boxes and old junk.

"That bastard next door, he had the mower going all morning. No respect for night workers, hey?"

The woman just stared back at him, trying to keep focus and not get distracted by potential escape routes. Rowan suddenly cupped his nose, face screwed up in disgust.

"Baby. Did you shit yourself?"

Tears started to run down her face.

"You haven't even had your coffee yet and your bowels are going," he joked.

"Can I go clean up?" the woman asked, embarrassed. "I don't want to sit in this mess."

Rowan took a sip of his drink, cupping the mug in his hands.

"I don't think so, not right now. We need a chat. I want to ask some questions."

"Rowan. Please..."

Another sip. Then he placed the mug down on the floor to one side.

"I guess my first question is an obvious one. I've asked it several times, and things just aren't making sense in my head."

The woman looked away, desperately calculating the best response to the situation.

"My question is... why? Why, baby?"

His wife didn't answer. She didn't even look at him.

Rowan wondered if she was thinking about the guy from her office, whether he might work out that something was wrong because of her radio silence. Maybe, just maybe, she was expecting an action film rescue, where he'd tear down into the room and fight Rowan for the ultimate prize... his wife.

The thought was hilarious.

"I can't stay down here, Rowan. Please. Let me go."

Rowan's eye twitched. He took another sip of coffee.

"Okay... I'll wait. That's a-okay. Don't forget I'm on the rota for overnights, so it will probably be a couple of days before our next opportunity to talk."

Rowan's face was blank, as if he were rehearsing some kind of script. His wife's face was the opposite. Crevices of panic ran across her face, alongside some developing crow's feet and wrinkles on her neck. She shuddered with anticipation of the nightmare to come.

"Okay, I'll talk. Ask me anything," she tried.

"It's okay, you're not ready. Anything you say now will be forced. I want you to *want* to tell me."

"I do," she begged, scraping herself onto her knees. "I'm so sorry, baby."

Rowan smiled. It was all a trick. He saw right through it.

He stood, grabbing the coffee mug on his ascent. Sighing, he started towards the door.

"ROWAN!" she shrieked, her mask slipping. "You can't leave!"

Rowan gestured towards the door with a confused look on his face.

"I'm not the one who's tied up, baby. Stop being silly. We'll talk later."

"I HAVE NO WATER! PLEASE!"

Rowan shuffled up the steps, completely unbothered.

"I'LL DIE DOWN HERE! ROWAN!"

He slammed the door shut and her voice disappeared instantly, as if it had been switched off. The basement was completely soundproof, working just as well as when he'd had it installed fifteen years ago.

On his phone, he pulled up a home security app, and loaded a video feed of the basement. There were three angles, the cameras hidden behind miscellaneous boxes and tools. He could see his wife on the floor, desperately flailing, trying to escape the restraints. Rowan wasn't stupid, and this wasn't his first rodeo. He'd tied her wrists with rope and clamped on a pair of cuffs too. He'd bought them for some fun in the bedroom, but it seemed like the basement was where the real action was happening.

The key to the cuffs was in a trashcan somewhere around Madison Street; he didn't bother noting down which one. Lies were all this woman knew, and any expectation on the contrary was foolish. He'd thrown the key away yesterday, when it was obvious his wife had become used to her snake-like ways. Days of questioning her in the basement, and nothing but bullshit in response.

She was going to rot under their family home. Gasping

with thirst, screaming as her organs shut down one by one. He wondered what her last thoughts would be...

Rowan thought this version of himself had been left firmly in the past. Ten years of marital bliss had settled his brain, cured his mental ailments. But the grotesque parts of him were rising to the surface, and he didn't feel equipped nor eager to push them back down.

The depot was quiet. Rowan got in and signed his paperwork in just a few minutes, which was far better than the half hour or so it usually took. The route tonight was an easy one—over to Egglemore, load up, and crash at a hotel. The next couple of days would be more full-on, but the pay was good so it was worth the time away from home. Plus, he'd have plenty of downtime between locations to watch his wife stew in her own filth. He hoped she'd last a while; it was far better entertainment than watching another random show on streaming.

Rowan nodded at another driver. He had plenty of casual acquaintances in the depot, and they were all as reserved and quiet as him. A simple nod or "hello" was as much socialising as he fancied most nights, but it kept things ticking along. The other driver headed out to his truck and did his checks. Rowan sipped from a polystyrene cup of instant coffee, drinking as much liquid caffeine as possible before a night on the road. When he was sure the coast was clear, Rowan opened up the home video app on his phone and smirked at the image.

His wife was screaming, and had obviously been doing so since he left the house. Her skin was flushed red, vocal cords straining aggressively. He didn't dare increase the volume, not in the depot. He'd do that on the road, use it as white noise to keep him awake in the darkness. With a tap of the screen, the angle changed, and he quickly cycled through each camera on repeat to get a good 360 degree view of the woman. A rumble in the distance alerted Rowan to another person coming into the depot, so he placed the device back in his jean pocket.

Another driver passed through. He got a nod, then Rowan got a move on. After routine checks to make sure the vehicle was safe to drive, he hopped into the driver's seat, and started on his way. At his first opportunity, he placed his phone in the mount and connected the aux, filling the cab with the shrieking cries of a dying woman.

Classical music had nothing on that symphony.

CHAPTER 14

CHARLES

The streets were alive in the evening. The main precinct buzzed with energy, happy hour signs plastered across the front of every bar. Crowds full of tech workers, office drones, and wealthy businessmen were packed into every establishment, spilling out onto the streets. Charles caught snippets of gossip, tearful phone calls, and hushed arguments on his way past the strip, directing himself towards the beach.

Though Charles had been living in *no fixed abode* for most of his adult life, he still had no real innate sense of direction. Everything was familiar, so to speak, but a lot of the connecting roads and parks were a blur. It kept things interesting in some ways; he could never really get bored of exploring the city.

Coloured lights refracted through steamy windows, beams of orange and pink dancing across the wet pavement. A storm was coming, that's what the radio said. The weather had been pretty temperate for late Autumn, and in a climate as mild as Egglemore's, it was rare to see more than a bit of thunder and lightning. But a full-on weather event was on its way, the likes of which most of the UK hadn't seen in decades.

The underpass would be fine for a night or so, but finding some proper shelter was going to be Charles' main priority. He had a couple of leads, potentially, from old friends and casual acquaintances. Rod had said that at a push, if he wanted to stay on the floor at the sandwich shop for a night or two, he was more than welcome. But Charles preferred not to put out his friends. He'd find somewhere else, and he had no doubt in his mind it would be perfect.

The beach was much quieter than the city centre. Waves caressed the shore, white foam settling on the pebbles. There was a gym on the seafront, a high-end but low traffic business, and if it was a particularly slow night, the manager usually let him in the changing rooms for a shower.

The glass-fronted building was tucked at the end of a quaint row of shops, all of which were shut for the day. Fluorescent lights beamed from a sign above the glass: *Rick's Workouts + Gym*. Through the window, Charles could only see two or three people using the machines, sweaty bodies looking strained and uncomfortable. It would be the perfect time to grab a quick wash.

Inside, a super-modern lobby led to an automated barrier, and it was here that Charles was stumped. These things were new, and without a membership card, he wouldn't be able to get face to face with any of the staff. Charles was much more charming in person, and though he could use the buzzer and talk to someone, it was much easier for them to wave him off that way. Especially if his usual contact wasn't on shift.

Damn.

Just behind him, lingering in the doorway, there was a man wearing a heavy raincoat, hood drawn up over his head, disguising his face. He leant against the wall, very potentially drunk if his posture was anything to go by.

"Hey," Charles called over. "Can you buzz me in? I left my card."

Ordinarily, he wouldn't have told a white lie, especially

such an implausible one. No-one would believe a man as scruffy as Charles had a membership to a high-end establishment like this one. But if the stranger was indeed a little intoxicated, it might be a harmless half-truth to get him to his hot shower.

Disappointingly, the man didn't answer. Instead, he just coughed, babbled under his breath and continued on his way, disappearing towards the beach.

Shit.

Out of options, Charles pressed the buzzer and tried to formulate the question in his head, leaving as little room for failure as possible. He really needed that shower. The smell coming from him was unnatural.

"Hi, are you having problems with the barrier?" a friendly male voice asked. It wasn't anyone Charles recognised, which was another hurdle.

"Hey, is Xander working tonight at all?"

The voice at the end of the line hesitated.

"He's not, no. Do you have a membership here?"

The receptionist must have looked at the camera. The shift in the tone of his voice was unmistakable.

"I'll level with you," Charles started. "I don't have a membership. I don't have a penny to my name. But sometimes when it's quiet I can get a shower here. I don't have anywhere else tonight."

More hesitance, but when the man responded, he had more humanity in his voice.

"I can get you in for fifteen, no worries. I'll buzz you in now, just come to reception when you're done."

"You're a star and a gentleman, thank you," Charles beamed, stepping through the barrier. He wiped his feet on the mat, and stepped into a long white hallway.

Inside the changing room, Charles peeled away the dirty clothes from his body. He had a change of underwear and socks in his bag, but he'd be replacing the rest of his outfit right after the shower.

The first step into the water was heaven. A blissful waterfall of warmth cascading down onto him. His body was marred with cuts and several rashes, dark skin mottled purple and red. Dripping from his shoulders, the water ran a murky brown, eventually washing away all the dirt and scum. Charles stood under it for a good ten minutes, increasing the heat until it was too much for him to handle.

He felt fresh, rejuvenated and ready to get back to his tent. With fresh underwear and socks on, Charles headed out to reception, expecting to find the owner of the male voice he talked to.

"I'm off now," he said to no-one, wondering if they might be just out of earshot. "Thank you again."

No answer.

Oh well. He'd note down *male voice* in his book. It would be hard to track anyone down from a voice alone, but he could revisit with a gift another time. Scratching the words into his notebook quickly, he headed back to the lobby, hoping he could exit without any fuss.

At the end of the white corridor, Charles could see a couple of shifting silhouettes. It was completely silent, but murmurs of their conversation were drifting in the air.

Apprehensively, he continued towards the exit, subconsciously treading quietly to avoid drawing any attention to himself. Charles heard one of the voices a little clearer.

"Is there anyone I can call for you?"

One of the fluorescents overhead started to flicker, diluting the flawless white decor with ugly grey shadows. The voice definitely belonged to the receptionist, and it sounded like he was trying to navigate a difficult situation.

"Sir, I'm going to have to ask you to stop walking into the barrier. It won't open without a membership card."

Suddenly, both of them came into view. The receptionist

was medium build, late 30s or so. And the other person was the raincoat guy from earlier. He was inside now, testing the receptionist's boundaries and patience, intermittently walking face-first into the barrier.

He was definitely drunk or on something.

Charles hung back, doing his best not to impose. He was in no real rush, and if he waited a bit he could thank the man who let him in.

Raincoat Guy walked into the barrier again, squashing his face against the glass. Incredibly, the man started to wail, a gruff distortion to his voice. Charles couldn't see all that well, but he imagined tears cascading down the clear plastic. The sound of his voice reverberating against the material was haunting in itself, but the complete lack of self-awareness was the real problem.

Charles had seen it all too much. High on drugs or drink, people became shadows of their former selves. They'd fight and argue and take stupid risks for the tiniest of rewards. It wasn't something he was immune to either—his past was blotted with shoplifting offences, petty theft, even minor assault. The Charles of today was not the Charles of yester-day, and as long as he worked hard on improving every single day, he could forgive himself for his less than stellar moments.

Eventually, he might even forgive himself for the biggest regret in his life.

But he wasn't there yet.

"Hey, is everything alright?" Charles asked, breaking the tension in the lobby. "I'm just out of the shower, so will be going now."

The receptionist looked back and seemed relieved to have another person with him.

"I'll buzz you back through," the receptionist said. "Just hang on one moment."

Charles did just that, watching the other man intently.

Living as Charles did heightened one's sensitivity to gut instinct, and something about this situation was making his belly turn.

Raincoat Guy continued wailing, bringing his head back and slamming it into the barrier. The receptionist was in over his head, and called for help on his radio. Charles felt a little useless, hanging back and observing, but it wasn't his place to intervene.

The wind was picking up outside, whipping a torrent of rain against the glass. A wet, teenage-looking man stepped inside, shaking water from his hair. Dressed in a black jacket with a clip-on radio hanging from the pocket, Charles guessed it was the complex security guard.

"What's going on mate?" he asked Raincoat Guy, nodding at the receptionist. "Gonna need you to leave if you're not a member."

Instead of listening,Raincoat Guy stared directly ahead, studying his reflection in the barrier. His face was uncovered slightly now, revealing an unkempt beard and a heavy nosebleed.

SLAM.

SLAM.

SLAM.

He wouldn't stop. Repeatedly smacking his face into the barrier, smashing up his flesh. The guard tried to intervene, but it was too late. Raincoat Guy pushed himself away from the plastic and turned to sprint away. Instead of the doorway, he collided with the window, and folded back to the tiled floor with a crunch.

The guard reached down to help him, but Raincoat Guy shifted across the floor to the corner, retreating like a caged animal. The hood had slipped now, and Charles could just about make out his face. It was flushed red with rage, cuts and bruises hatched across his left cheek and forehead.

Charles looked for any other exits. He didn't want to leave

these people in their moment of need, but getting involved in anything like this never worked in his favour. Whilst he considered his options, the receptionist quickly leant over the barrier and took out a jangle of keys, unlocking the gate. It swiped open, and there was almost no obstacle between Charles and the scuffle.

"Get out of here!" the security guard wailed, his voice breaking in a panic. It was unlikely he'd experienced too much of this nonsense at this end of town; his usual day probably consisted of handling self-entitled Karens and obnoxious businessmen, not aggressive drunks.

With barely a moment to think, the guard was overcome by Raincoat Guy's strength. In a swift but clumsy motion, he pounced and tackled the guard to the floor, before pummelling scrunched up fists into his face. The receptionist sprinted over and tried to pull the crazed man away, but it was too late.

Raincoat Guy bit the guard on the cheek, drawing blood effortlessly as he sunk his teeth into the skin. He tossed his head side-to-side like a dog with a squeaky toy, and pulled a chunk out of his face. The receptionist froze in his spot, suddenly unable to move. Raincoat Guy spat out the mangled flesh and twisted to look at the scared man.

"Move!" Charles screamed, sprinting towards the scene. He shouldered the receptionist out of the way just as Raincoat Guy was about to make contact. With a soft crunch, the receptionist slid across the floor, away from the action, and Charles collided with the deranged man.

They collapsed in a heap, and Charles felt a muscle in his right shoulder pop. Straining to keep the man off of him, Charles quickly twisted to get on top. Raincoat Guy snarled, red-brown teeth snapping in a frenzied attack. Thinking on his toes, Charles swung the messenger bag in between him and the man and pushed down to smother him.

A wailing siren blared outside the gym and two police

officers quickly filtered through the door. Charles jumped away at the last minute and was relieved to see the man still breathing. As he stumbled upright, shoulder in red-hot agony, Raincoat Guy thrashed and squealed until the police had him cuffed and restrained. One of them, a female officer with a scar across her eye, turned to talk to Charles.

"You'll both need to get to the hospital as soon as possible," she said. "Are you injured?"

"No, I'm not. But he is—"

Charles pointed to the guard, who was writhing in silent pain, blood spurting from the wound on his face. His outline was traced by a growing pool of crimson.

"Okay. Get out of here, and get to a doctor as soon as you can."

The other police officer was struggling to keep the man contained. With a friendly but obviously strained smile, the female officer turned to help him and dragged Raincoat Guy from the building. Moments later, an ambulance pulled up and tended to the guard.

"You saved my life," the receptionist whispered. "I don't understand—"

The receptionist was as pale as a ghost, his freshly-shaven face nearly translucent.

"It was nothing," Charles said. "I was going to thank you for the shower."

The receptionist's eyes trailed to Charles' brown leather jacket. It was covered in blood, which had splattered across his neck and face.

"Do you need another one?" he asked.

Charles looked down too.

"I might take you up on that."

The receptionist escorted him back through the barrier, offering a cup of tea as well as a whole half hour in the changing room. Charles wasn't going to say no to either of those things.

He stripped down, placing his items in a locker. Before heading to the shower, he grabbed his notepad from his bag and unclipped the pen from the front. On the most recent page, Charles crossed out his entry for *"male voice"*—he considered the receptionist's good faith well and truly repaid.

He had the aching shoulder to prove it.

CHAPTER 15

MAGGIE

Maggie and Claire sauntered down the hallway, back towards the lifts. It was nearly 9pm now, many, many hours later than either of them had wanted to stay, but they were in good spirits, talking and joking. There was nothing more annoying than driving back home in the dark, but Maggie was confident that the tests and insight into Claire's condition were worth it.

"Can we get dinner on the way home?" Claire asked.

Maggie nodded.

"There's a drive-thru down the road. We'll get burgers if you want."

Claire smiled enthusiastically.

"You know I do."

Claire hit the button to call the elevators. When the metal doors opened a few moments later, Maggie noticed an elderly woman slumped against the wall inside, the mirrored glass reflecting her image. Maggie recognised her as the one trapped in the car earlier, with the unusual eyes and possible dementia.

"Hey, are you okay?" Claire asked. Maggie stood still,

unwilling to enter the shaft until the woman turned to face them.

The woman didn't answer. Didn't move a muscle.

BLEEEP.

The hospital tannoy crackled into life, and a panicked woman's voice bounced around the speakers in the ceiling.

"Will all visitors please report to reception immediately via Hallway B. This hospital is entering lockdown in line with the NHS lockdown procedure. Do NOT use the lifts, please only use the stairs. I repeat, will all visitors—"

"HAAAAAAAARHGGGG!"

The elderly woman twisted, snapping to face them with a gargled wail. She scurried across the elevator floor, bones grinding together with each movement, arms flailing.

With a friendly *beep*, the doors to the escalator slid shut, closing on one of the woman's wrinkly hands. Her spindly fingers crunched on impact and the lift call light in the corridor turned red. The fingers writhed between the crushing metal before she eventually dragged them back in, skin degloving in a sickly motion. A mess of torn, thin flesh slopped out onto the corridor floor, right by Maggie's feet.

"What's happening?" Claire screamed, backing away from the lift. Maggie was focusing on trying to find a way out, eyes darting from door to door, praying for an exit.

"Over there!"

Maggie grabbed Claire's arm and paced towards a fire exit marked by an illuminated sign. She forced the push-handle, and a gust of air swept the door open, clanging it against a metal guardrail. Cascading levels of stairs descended to street level, sketchily bolted onto the exterior brickwork. A young girl stood immediately outside the door, causing Maggie and Claire to jump backwards. Maggie noticed her demeanour, her sunken, rage-filled eyes, and quickly grabbed for the handle.

"Mum!" Claire shouted.

The girl burst forward, grabbing Maggie by her jumper, trying to pull her outside.

"Get off of me!"

Maggie forced a flat palm into the girl's chest, knocking her backwards, and by the time the door was shut, she could hear the girl tumbling down the stairs outside.

"We need to get out of here. Right now!" Maggie ordered, leading Claire to the interior stairwell. God only knew what was going on, but if it was a lockdown, it was serious.

They ran down as fast as they could, a blur of signs and posters whipping past. At ground level, Maggie quickly darted to each signboard, looking for a way out. The crowd on the stairwell behind them was growing, a wave of panicked visitors rushing to leave.

The tannoy announcement was playing on a loop. The signs were almost unreadable, a confusing vomit of arrows and colours and department names. Maggie had no idea what was going on, but couldn't take her mind off of the elderly woman. The way her skin slurried from her fingers without as much as a groan.

Focus.

The reception was a no-go. If they went there, they'd be kettled until the early hours, at least. This place wasn't safe for her, and it wasn't safe for Claire. Claire already seemed stressed and disoriented (why wouldn't she?) so it was in both of their best interests to get out of this hospital, and then Egglemore as a whole. There was only one direction to go from the stairwell: through the hall and out into another, bigger corridor.

"Move!"

A scruffy twentysomething slammed into Claire, knocking her to the floor. Her phone tumbled from her hand, shattering the screen.

"HEY!" Maggie called out, grabbing the man by the collar of his hoodie. She tightened both hands around the material, scrunching up his face. "Watch where the fuck you're going."

She held him there for a moment, staring into his eyes.

"I'm sorry, miss—"

Claire got up, brushing herself off. The parade of people kept churning through into the hallway.

"Mum?"

Maggie forced him away from her, and he bounced hard off the wall, before sprinting to catch up with his friends.

"He broke my phone," Claire said, her teenage priorities right where Maggie expected them to be.

"We'll get it fixed. Come on."

They joined the crowd, moving as one entity through the hallway. People were making calls, frantically searching their handbags for keys, muttering questions aloud to themselves, bewildered by the situation.

Maggie wanted to be at the front. She couldn't let them get trapped in this place.

With Claire's hand in hers, she started to squeeze through the gaps, driving forward with her shoulder to make space. Maggie wasn't a small woman, far from it, and her size was helping part the crowd. Claire followed close, leaning through the space her mum was making.

They were approaching the end of the hallway. Two double doors, then if Maggie remembered right, a couple of left turns to get back to reception. She had no intention of staying inside the building, and if anyone tried to make her, they'd learn what it felt like to be on her bad side.

"Mum, slow down!"

"Not far now," Maggie groaned, aware that Claire probably couldn't hear her.

The crowd was only a hundred metres or so behind them, and Maggie had finally reached the front. Out of breath, and sweat dripping from everywhere, she charged forward, blocking anyone from getting ahead of her.

From around the corner, the security guard from earlier stumbled into view. He was holding his neck, blood staining his skin and jacket.

"Stop!" he called out, croaking through his injury. "You can't come this way!"

Fifty or so people were surging towards the exit, and it was an accident waiting to happen. Deflated, he grabbed his radio and muttered some unintelligible words before stepping back around the corner.

Without warning, the double doors slammed shut, some kind of mechanism kicking into action remotely.

"No!" Maggie called out, still running at full speed. She turned her head, saw the rush of people behind her. "Everyone stop! The doors are closed!"

Instinctively, she pulled Claire in front of her and piled into the corner, head down to protect them both. They stayed this way, wrapped against the tiny wall, as the mass of people crashed into the doors, barely moving them an inch.

They were specially designed lockdown doors, Maggie pondered, tracing her thoughts for some kind of helpful information. With a career background in IT security systems, this was something she might well have an upper hand in.

In the old days, as Claire liked to call it, Maggie had built a business from scratch, installing custom-built IT systems for a variety of different clients. These ranged from basic payroll and company software all the way through to complex security systems, including the ones the NHS used. As far as she knew, the same systems were still in use today. Maggie had sold the business with high hopes her work would remain helpful for decades, but the new owners cut every cost possible to increase profits. Another day, another greedy capitalist.

True, she made a killing from selling the company, but she didn't see herself as one of *them*. She spent her days now trying to be helpful, participating in hackathons and similar events to keep her money and skills ticking over. If only she'd decided to spend some of that money going private instead of waiting for an appointment at Egglemore.

Maggie straightened up from her cradling position, and looked around. The hallway was packed, bodies shoving bodies in riotous fits of panic. A dozen or so people were on their phones, talking to loved ones or the police or whoever they could reach. The rest looked as if they were losing their minds.

"Everyone stop!" she shouted out. "They won't let us out unless we calm down!"

Claire was flushed red, tears bubbling in her eyes. Maggie held her hand as she addressed the crowd. As she looked over behind them, she noticed the doors at the other end of the corridor were sealed shut too.

"They can't do this to us!" one person cried.

"I'm suing the Hell out of them for this!" another said.

Maggie rolled her eyes and pulled out her phone, keeping Claire hidden behind her. She didn't want things to descend into violence, but it was foolish to think it wouldn't.

On-screen, she brought up an app and typed in some credentials. She'd built her own interface to navigate the software suites she'd developed, and even though she didn't have control of it all anymore, it was likely she could find a way in.

Big business was lazy like that. They wouldn't bother keeping the code up to date and would only do an overhaul if one day things went bang.

"What are we going to do?" Claire asked, her face wet with tears. Maggie turned towards her.

"I tell you what we're *not* going to do," Maggie started. "And that's panic. I think I can get us out."

"How?" Claire moaned.

"Give me two minutes."

Maggie tapped and typed, the complex code second nature to her.

"I can get these doors unlocked. Is anyone speaking to the reception?" Maggie asked. Most of them ignored her, and a couple just shook their heads.

Maggie scrolled into a blueprint of the hospital, which was dotted with sensor locations and exits. After some more tapping, the doors unlocked with a pneumatic hiss. Maggie pushed them open and dragged Claire into the next corridor.

"How did you get through? Get back right now!" the guard ordered, running over from another room. He got right up into Maggie's face and she just smirked.

"I owe you a punch in the face for leaving me and my daughter trapped in there. Do you want it now or later?"

The guard scowled, his brow darkening.

"That's what I thought," Maggie said. "Now tell me, how do we get out of here?"

The guard brought his hand away from his neck for the first time in the conversation. A deep gash was oozing with blood and some unidentifiable clear liquid.

"You think I don't want to get out of here too?"

Maggie scoffed.

"With that injury, I'd say you're right where you need to be. But we aren't… So tell me how to get out."

The man started to scratch around the wound. A pinprick rash was developing at the edges of the laceration.

"We've gone into a full shutdown. There's no way in or out aside from the fire exits."

"And where is the nearest one?"

The guard scowled again, obviously hoping Maggie would back down. Defeated, he turned to point at the room he came from.

"In there. That room has an exit in the far corner."

"Right. Thanks very much," she said, pushing past him.

Claire hurried behind, fearfully remaining only a pace or two behind Maggie at all times.

"When we get out there, stay right by me, okay?"

Maggie walked in, scanning the room for the door. But there was nothing there.

No kind of opening. No fire exit.

As she turned back, she saw the guard quickly locking the door they entered through.

"What the fuck are you doing?"

Breaking her hand away from Claire's, Maggie marched up to the door. There was a square safety window framed by thick wood. The rest of the door was reinforced.

"It's for your own safety," the security guard huffed, before noticing the onslaught of visitors pouring from the other corridor. He ran to intercept them.

"FUCK!" Maggie snapped, kicking a table leg. "This fucking place."

CHAPTER 16
TODD

Todd and his Gran ate leftovers whilst staring out of his bedroom window. The estate was buzzing with activity, everyone out on the walkways outside their front doors, an audience spanning ten floors. Paramedics and police rushed around like worker ants, trying to contain the deadly scene on the ground. It was way past midnight, but there wouldn't be much sleep happening for anyone tonight.

The guy that bit the fireman was still trapped on the balcony outside his house. Todd could see him flailing up there, completely ignorant of what he'd done. The way the flats were set out, each floor had a balcony running end to end, providing a walkway to the front doors. These were interspersed with stairwells that ran top to bottom, usually in the middle of the structure. The fifth floor balcony serviced around fifteen houses, but only the deranged businessman was out front. Any other occupants were probably hiding inside, watching things unfold from behind the safety of their windows.

As if reading Todd's mind, the businessman started sprinting up and down the balcony, slamming on windows and trying to force himself through the doors.

"Why aren't the police trying to stop him?" his Gran asked.

"Probably bigger fish to fry down there," Todd answered matter of factly.

Their vantage point didn't offer much of a perspective of the ground level. Part of him wanted to sneak out and check out the scene. A bigger part of him thought that was a horrendous idea. Besides the dead body and a whole lot of blood, there were too many strangers out there. How was he to know who might go crazy next?

It seemed like such a random attack, frenzied even, and Todd's mind was racing with fearful possibilities. Was it another pandemic waiting to happen? Some kind of illness?

Too many questions, not enough answers.

Todd had messaged the girl from before —Tanya— to see if she had any updates, but she'd stopped replying a while ago. When it was safe to do so again, he'd fly the drone out and check on her window. There was no way on God's Earth he was going out there himself.

"I should check on Benjamin," his gran asked.

"What?"

Todd stopped eating, dropping his cutlery into the bowl.

"Well, he looked tired and—"

"Are you crushing on him, Gran?"

"Oh don't be such a stupid idiot."

"You know you're allowed to. You have my blessing."

His Gran put her bowl on the table and placed her tightly-curled fists on her hips.

"As if I'd ask you for your bloody blessings anyway, you idiot!"

Todd smirked.

"Gran and Benjamin, sitting up a tree—"

"Oh grow up you silly fucker. You're twenty-five, not five!"

Todd pulled the curtain shut.

"And you're seventy five plus the rest, so it's bedtime for you."

Her mouth dropped.

"I'll have you know—"

Todd grabbed her bowl and playfully escorted her out to the kitchen. He pushed gently on her back to speed her up.

"I can't believe you! All that going on out there, and you're treating me like this," she complained.

Todd giggled. His Gran definitely missed her calling, he thought, with the theatrical flair she brought to every situation. She was destined for the stage or screen.

"Right, night, see you in the morning, have a good one, love you," he blurted, waving and sprinting back into his room. He heard her complain through the door.

"I'm sorry, was I holding you up from something? Better not be watching pornography in there, Todd!"

Todd rolled his eyes and opened his laptop. He went straight to his browser and typed a rotating selection of words in the search bar.

"Egglemore"
"Egglemore emergency"
"Egglemore police"
"Egglemore news"

A variety of articles popped up on-screen, all small, local publications. None of the national sites had posted much about Egglemore at all, aside from the weather warnings. Todd stretched out his neck, pushing on his chin, then pulled out his phone.

Still no messages.

"Benjamin?" he heard his Gran say in the kitchen. She was already calling him after two seconds alone. Definitely a crush. Todd could put matchmaker on his CV now.

The drone was out of battery again, so he grabbed it from the side and plugged it into the outlet. Todd was desperate to check on Tanya. She lived directly underneath the rabid businessman in the adjacent block, and it was only a matter of time until he left the balcony and went exploring. The stairwell was accessible twenty-four hours a day, and from what he could see, no-one had sectioned it off.

The complex felt too quiet. An ominous silence pervaded. Blue and red lights beamed from the emergency vehicles on the ground, intermittently drowning Todd's bedroom in a blue and red wash. A torrent of rain splattered across the window, roaring winds surging through the estate—the only thing to break the quiet. Most people were back in their homes now, cosy tungsten rooms in stark contrast to the inky sky.

"Benjamin?" he heard his Gran call again. Todd drowned out her voice and focused on the laptop. He had to find out more information. His anxiety was through the roof.

Without warning, his phone started to vibrate.

"Tanya?" he asked silently and hopefully. That hope was short-lived when a haunting siren started to sound from the device. Todd snatched his phone, and read the bright red notification pulsating on screen. It was an emergency alert, a few lines of text written in capital letters.

"EMERGENCY ALERT. Stay in your homes. Immediate curfew order is in action until further notice."

Todd's heart was racing. As soon as he dismissed the notification, he heard the same siren blaring on his Gran's phone in the other room.

"Gran? Did you just get the alert?"

He twisted the handle and snatched open the door. His Gran stood at the entrance to the flat, which opened directly into the kitchen. Benjamin was at the threshold, his hair messy and clothes disheveled. Todd recognised the smart casualwear from his visit earlier in the evening. He hadn't changed his clothes, but had definitely slept. That was a bedhead if ever he'd seen one.

"Benjamin, what are you doing here? I thought you were off to bed," his Gran said. "You look really tired."

Benjamin was hunched up and bent slightly forward, mumbling something under his breath. Each second that passed saw him stumble slightly further into the flat. His Gran took several gentle paces backwards.

"Take a seat. Are you hungry? You don't look so well."

Gran glanced over at Todd, confusion written on her face.

"Hi, Benjamin? Everything alright mate?" Todd asked. The elderly man paid him no mind, his eyes locked straight forward.

Gran pulled out a chair at the kitchen table and gestured towards Benjamin to sit down.

He didn't sit.

Instead, his face contorted into something almost inhuman. His eyes scrunched up, deep wrinkles set like scars. His mouth opened wide, a cavernous abyss.

And then he screamed, a croaky, wet, guttural sound exploding from his chest. Rage surged through his body as he pounced, taking flight in a brutal tackle that defied his age. He careened into the elderly woman, knocking her into the table. Her back folded the wrong way, crunching on impact, before they spilled onto the floor.

Todd's anxiety bled into anger. A kickstart of adrenaline raced through his veins as he burst into action without even thinking, launching his lean frame into the pensioner. The momentum tore Benjamin's grip away from Gran and Todd was already back on his feet, grappling with him.

"Stop right now!" Todd screamed. Benjamin's face transformed from sorrow to sick joy as he flopped around, trying to wriggle away. Todd slammed his fist into Benjamin's stomach, hoping to temporarily impair him. But it didn't work. Instead, he gargled and spat, putrid fluid frothing from his lips.

"Benjamin! Fucking stop!"

The elderly man launched himself, throwing Todd from him like a ragdoll. His strength was implausible, as was his newfound agility. The wear and tear evident in his normal pained shuffling around the estate had disappeared. Needles of pain shot through Todd's back as he collided with the floor, and by the time he'd stilled from the motion, Benjamin was back above him, ready to attack.

With a spring-like action, Todd kicked his legs out and booted Benjamin square in the kneecap. His bone snapped, causing him to crumple back to the ground.

"Stop it, you two!" Todd's Gran screamed. She limped over to the rage-driven man, and leant over him caringly. "Please tell us what's wrong!"

Benjamin's head snapped to the side, and within moments, he'd wrapped his fingers around the woman's ankle. He sank his teeth into her thin skin and ripped out a mouthful of flesh. Todd's Gran squealed in pain, stumbling back onto the dining chair.

"What the fuck?" Todd screamed.

Todd pounced, closing the gap between him and Benjamin. With brutal force, he kicked the elderly man square in the face. His head snapped on tiled floor and knocked him out cold.

"Gran!"

Todd ran over to her, swiping a tea towel from the counter. With rudimentary handiwork, he wrapped the cloth around the wound, tying it firmly. By the time the wound was covered, it had already bled through the fabric, oozing through the fibres.

"I just need my phone, one second."

Todd crashed through his door and grabbed his phone. He had three missed notifications from Tanya. She'd have to wait.

With trembling fingers, he dialled the emergency services. The line was engaged.

"What the fuck is happening?" Todd asked. His heart was beating hard. Sweat trickled from his forehead. The situation was catching up with him, fast.

Back in the kitchen, he grabbed another tea towel from the cupboard.

"No, no, not that one," his Gran moaned. "Use one of the crusty ones, not my Jubilee specials."

Forever protective of anything related to the Royal Family, using one of her Queen's Jubilee towels would be impertinent.

Frustrated, Todd grabbed the stack of towels from the cupboard and chucked them on the table. His Gran picked out one she wouldn't mind getting filthy.

"Aaaah!" she screamed, as Todd rewrapped the makeshift bandage.

"Sorry, hold still."

There was so much blood.

"Fuck, fuck." Todd's mind was spinning. His motions were jerky, desperate. "I need to—"

His throat felt as if it was closing up. He needed to breathe.

Four things you can see.

Three things you can hear.

Two things you can feel.

The emergency line was still engaged. Another round of alerts buzzed through to their phones, grinding vibrations swallowed by an even louder, tinny siren.

"Why aren't they fucking answering?"

Todd's Gran placed her hand on his shoulder, an age-old trick to calm him down if he got too flustered.

"I'm okay. Get me a tea. That will spark me up whilst we wait."

She smiled through the pain, but he could tell she was flagging. Her skin was getting paler. She couldn't sit up straight, something displaced bulging in her back. Todd span round to the counter and switched on the kettle. Every movement felt out-of-body, like someone else was controlling his actions.

Benjamin was still unconscious. Todd couldn't ponder anything other than that for the moment. Facing the fact he'd kicked a lovely old man full pelt in the head wouldn't make any of this better right now.

He absent-mindedly ran through the routine. Teabag. Sugar (*three, because she didn't really like the taste of tea*). Plenty of milk.

A harrowing scream echoed through the complex, followed by a crushing sound. It didn't even register in Todd's mind. He plunked the tea down by his Gran and tried his phone again three times. The television was on. Todd hadn't noticed before. The shows were carrying on as usual, late-night reruns for the elderly and the insomniacs.

Todd's Gran sipped her tea, then smacked it back down on the table. Lunging, she grabbed at her ankle, compressing the wound under the bandage. Tears trickled from her face.

Do something, Todd.

He turned back round and paced to the cupboard. Shelves of miscellaneous food and medical supplies. Tablets. Painkillers. One of them should help.

"Take a few of these," he muttered, popping ibuprofen from its blister packaging. His mind was dull, unresponsive. He couldn't get a hold of his thoughts.

The sound from the TV speakers seemed obnoxiously loud in the otherwise silent room.

"I'm gonna go down there," Todd said, almost choking on the reality of those words. There was nothing he wanted less than to go out into the darkness, leaving his Gran bleeding out. But how else would he find a medic?

"Todd, I'm okay," his Gran said. "Don't be putting yourself in danger for me."

He shook his head.

"No. They're not answering, and we need help. They're just down there. I'll be careful."

Before he could change his mind, he grabbed his coat.

"Can you help me to my room before you go? I'm going to have a nap."

Todd stopped to look at her.

"Is that a good idea? You might be concussed."

She nodded.

"And do something about him, won't you? I don't want him in my house."

Todd hadn't even considered Benjamin. He was still lying there in the middle of the floor.

With gritted teeth, he helped his Gran into her small box room. She flopped onto the bed, immediately staining the sheets dark crimson. He wouldn't mention that right now, for fear of her trying to do a full load of washing with a gammy leg whilst he was out.

"Here's some water. If you feel funny, don't go to sleep, okay?"

His Gran laughed.

"I've woken up thousands of times, love, don't worry about me. I'm quite good at it."

Todd rolled his eyes and gave her a kiss on the head. Then he rushed back out to the living room. With an awkward heave, he dragged Benjamin to the door, careful not to bash his head around too much more.

With a final pull, he slipped the man over the threshold and onto the balcony. He'd already messed with the scene of the crime; it was probably best not to drag him too much further out. Just enough to keep his Gran safe for a moment.

As he stood up, Todd seized in pain, a static jolt running through his back.

He was midway through a probable fibromyalgia diagnosis and had made disappointingly little progress in finding ways to manage the pain. He'd always been fit, and doing fitness from home as a job helped keep him flexible and strong. But the waves of drowsiness and inexplicable pain always found a way to surprise him, and also liked to appear at the most inconvenient of times. Right now was one of them.

"Need a hand with that?" someone asked.

A woman's voice.

Todd turned to look at the stranger.

It was Tanya from the other block. Her hair was dishevelled, as if it had been a bit of a journey to get there, yet she was glorious to behold.

"Yes please," he answered, relieved.

CHAPTER 17
ALICE

The taxi never arrived.

But the barebones of a police cordon did, right around 7:00pm. By 10:00pm, barriers were erected around the entire perimeter of the service station, with considerable police presence. From what she could see in the darkness, the motorway was still open, as was the first access road into the complex. But any chance of her getting to Egglemore that night was wishful thinking.

She had tried calling everyone she could think of to get her out. Friends, acquaintances, even old colleagues from a few towns over. But the consensus was obvious. There was no getting in or out of Egglemore in the immediate future.

That also meant the meeting was off. She'd travelled to meet a contact, who said she had a story that would blow one dodgy company wide open. It was the story Alice needed, the story she'd dreamt of getting for over a decade. Something to really put her on the map, a proper job writing proper articles.

At least something was happening here. Something volatile and interesting. Alice was going to get to the bottom of it; it was too good to leave on the table.

Rhys, the brown-haired, surviving member of the coach brother duo, was sitting over the table from Alice, looking at something on his phone.

"The internet's out now too," he said, his words tinged with melancholy.

Everyone's phones had stopped working shortly after the cordon was in place outside. It was obvious the cell signal had been compromised in the area. Perhaps it was hackers, but more probably it was the government. They always had their hands in this kind of thing.

Alice hadn't managed to send or receive a single text message for hours, let alone make a call. It was the first time in a long time she'd felt truly disconnected from the world. If not for the pressing meeting she was scrambling to rearrange, it would have been quite peaceful, actually.

The service station exits had been secured. A half dozen officers were working to ensure it stayed that way. At a guess, there were a couple of hundred people spotted around the sprawling building. The rest had been lucky and escaped to their cars before the perimeter was put up. Alice even spoke to a few people who had been abandoned by their friends and family in the panic, only to have no way of contacting or getting back to them.

She was stressed and impatient and over the whole situation.

"We need to find a way out of here," she murmured to Rhys, catching his attention. "I can't stay like this all night."

The police hadn't even arranged rooms at the motel quite literally adjacent to the building. They were being kept like caged animals in a capitalist nightmare, overwhelmed by primary colours and fast-food slogans. The only silver lining (if that's what you could call it) was that the workers were also trapped in with them, and had been kind enough to keep making coffee and food. They were still taking full payments for it all though, so it was hardly a thoughtful gesture.

"There's no way out. There's police everywhere," Rhys sighed.

"There's always a way. I'm going to scope it out. Coming?"

Rhys nodded, grabbing his half-empty bottle of cloudy lemonade from earlier and swigging it down in one.

"I need to get to the hospital to see Jake. Can you take me there?"

Rhys's brother had been packed into an ambulance before the place had been locked down, but whether he had made it to the hospital was anyone's guess. If the wider world looked anything like it did in the courtyard right now, it wasn't hopeful.

Alice agreed to take him, but had no real intention of doing so. She had her own plans to take care of. Another pair of hands would be helpful in escaping the building, but when they were past the cordon outside, she'd be flying solo.

The immediate vicinity consisted of rows of tables and chairs, arranged in a sporadic, contemporary layout. A handful of fast food outlets ran around the perimeter, with toilets and washroom facilities at the end of a separate corridor. The chicken vendor (*Hot Chick Delight*) was the only one shuttered, due to the boiling oil situation earlier in the day. A salad bar and burger chain rounded off the food options.

"We need to check the exits people are least likely to use," Alice whispered to Rhys. "Any kind of management office, janitor closet, staff room. Things like that."

They both headed around the final vendor and into the long corridor. One wall was painted vomit orange, the opposite one adorned with large somewhat pixelated photographs of the local area. The décor left a lot to be desired. A smattering of gumball machines and ATMs led the way to the first room.

"This one?" Rhys asked.

"We'll give it a go."

Alice looked over her shoulder. There were a few people dawdling around at the opposite end of the hall, but nothing to be concerned about. She quickly tried the handle, but it was locked.

"Shit," Rhys said, despondent already.

"Let's try some others. We can always look for a key to this one later."

Several more doors lined the hallway, and the third one they tried opened up into a small wash closet. A variety of cleaning products were stacked on floor-to-ceiling shelves, faded signage indicating procedures and hazards. Aside from these items, there was nothing to see. The walls were thick breezeblock, sealed shut with just the one entrance and exit.

"What are you doing?"

It was the elderly woman from earlier, dragging her injured and just as elderly husband around like a dog.

Alice turned and smiled.

"Getting out of here. What about you?"

"There's no way out. Police at every exit—"

"I know that," Alice said. "But I'm getting out either way. Coming with us or not?"

Moments later, the couple were off searching for a key for the first room, whilst Alice and Rhys tried the final door in the corridor.

"Here goes nothing..." Rhys mumbled, pushing on the door. A wave of putrid air rushed from the room, as if finally being set free after decades. Alice and Rhys covered their mouths instinctively, gagging at the smell.

It was another, larger closet stocked with similar items to the last one, plus mops, brooms, and larger industrial tools. But smack bang in the middle of the floor, abandoned in a shallow puddle of blue bleach, was the melted boy from earlier. The parts of him that weren't still in the deep fat fryer or glued to the floor in the main lobby were liquified, a soupy porridge of flesh. His entire right arm, face, and most of his chest were melted, the fabric of his clothes fused to the skin. It was obvious that someone had tried to use the cleaning products on his corpse to hide the smell, but that had just escalated his decomposition.

Tears filled Alice's eyes. Not because she was upset, but due to the ungodly scent emanating from the heaped pile. Quickly scanning the room for a door, she slammed it back shut when it was evident there was no exit there.

"Well that's fucking disgusting," Rhys gagged.

"Yeah, let's not open that one again. We'll try the second floor whilst we wait for the others."

CHAPTER 18

ROWAN

The truck was pulled up on the side of the motorway. Rowan had a frozen meal in the microwave, which was accessible via a panel in the overhead shelving unit. Coffee was brewing in the cheap but reliable cafetière the next unit over. It was a compact and comfortable setup, largely the same in every truck Rowan had used in his twenty-year career.

A little later, he was enjoying tikka masala and a black coffee, eyes glued to his phone. Wind whipped past the vehicle, and a torrent of rain soon followed. The weather was particularly tricky at this time of year, when the area was prone to wind and heavy rainfall. The fact a major storm had been announced made it that much more treacherous.

Between spoonfuls of creamy curry, Rowan opened up his home security app. It was time to check on his darling.

His wife was bent forward, trying to sleep. Every time she drifted off, her arms would contort and pull on the restraints. It was like watching a dog try and stay awake: largely entertaining but he wanted more.

At the time of setting the cameras up, Rowan hadn't realised there was an interface to talk to (well, *through*) the camera. He'd only discovered it by accident one day when messing around with his phone. He decided that a little one-on-one time would be good for him and his wife.

He tapped the mic button and started talking.

"Hi baby, how are you doing?"

The voice lagged on-screen, but the woman's reaction made it obvious he'd been heard, loud and clear.

"ROWAN? ROWAN CAN YOU HEAR ME?"

Rowan chuckled.

"I can. Are you behaving?"

"FUCK YOU! ARE YOU WATCHING ME?"

"I am. I'm just having a snack and some coffee. You look beautiful in that light, you know that, love?"

"I AM GOING TO KILL YOU! I'LL END YOU!"

Rowan smirked.

"You're a very angry person. Surely, it's *me* that should be angry?"

His wife didn't respond. She was being coy.

"Well, if you don't want to talk, I'll leave you to it."

That perked her up.

"No, no. Rowan... I need some water. Please come get me out."

Rowan ate the last spoonful of his dinner and stashed the empty packaging in a black trash bag.

"Okay. You know, maybe this has gotten out of hand," he said into his phone mic. "Maybe I can come get you. I just need one thing from you first..."

"What is it?" she asked, her mouth taking on some kind of badly dubbed effect with the camera lag.

"I want to know his name."

His wife was still looking at the camera, but seemed to have frozen. It wasn't a technology issue though. No, this was a truth issue. She was trying to take him as a fool again, he could just feel it.

"Pretending to freeze up won't change my mind," he

scoffed, slurping his coffee. It was bitter, almost undrinkable. Just how he liked it.

"And… if I give you his name, that will be the end of it? You'll come get me?"

Rowan rolled his eyes with the full knowledge that she couldn't see him. He had the power in this situation. He always had the power, even when people tried to fuck him around.

"Sure, sure, love. I just need to know that one small tidbit of information. Then I'll turn right back round for you."

She stared into the camera, appearing as a frail, broken woman in the modestly-sized phone screen.

"Okay. Baby I love you. I'll—"

Suddenly, the phone went black. A buffering graphic popped up on-screen, but it didn't load anything.

"Shit," he sighed.

Oh well. He'd check in with her later. It appeared as if the entire cellular network had just gone down. He couldn't load text messages, the internet, or even get a dial tone. Weird. Rowan would often lose signal on the road, and the internet was spotty anywhere outside the big cities. But for everything to stop working in tandem was a bigger issue. Hopefully, just a glitch. He didn't want to lose precious time watching his wife rot. He had a few more games he wanted to play with her before she expired.

Dinner and coffee done, he tidied his dashboard and got back on the road. It was eerily quiet on the motorway. Sure, it was the early hours of the morning, but it was very rare not to see at least a handful of vehicles on the stretch. He wasn't going to question it, though—it meant he might even get ahead of his day.

Streetlamps dashed past the windscreen; the only thing visible aside from the beams of his headlights on the road. Puddles were starting to form from the rain, the road surface becoming increasingly slippery and treacherous. Rowan pulled back to fifty miles an hour to alleviate the risk, and coasted down the never-ending, rolling abyss.

Whilst he drove, he listened to podcasts. He wasn't a true crime junkie or a romance lover; he preferred nonfiction topics. Self-help, how to be successful, all that stuff. Today's listening material covered the basics of confidence, how to be a better you, and dealing with failure. He loved to soak himself in knowledge and work out how to apply said knowledge to his own situation.

"The thing about confidence is that it's a fickle beast. Some situations are easy to navigate. Social situations with family and friends. A discussion with work colleagues… But the scenarios that bring out our innermost fears are those which are foreign to us. Think back to a time when someone hurt you. Think about all the ways you allowed their actions to change the way you move in the world. Why is it that when other people hurt us, we retreat and become a shell of our former selves, but they get to continue on with a newfound energy and sense of self?"

Rowan nodded along, as if every point was customised just for his listening pleasure. He saw a lot of his past in the advice the deep-voiced narrator boomed. And a little bit of his present, too.

As he pondered life lessons and the meaning of *taking life into your own hands,* a figure appeared a few hundred metres down the road. The silhouette of a person, barely visible in dark clothes and bearing no kind of light. The idiot was stumbling around in the middle of the lane, completely ignorant to the fact a ten thousand-pound vehicle was hurtling towards him, with no real option to stop suddenly.

Of course, he didn't have to stop at all. An HGV driving at fifty miles an hour had a greatly increased stopping distance compared to a car or consumer vehicle. It would be well within the realm of truth to say he didn't even see the person in the road. Any jury would sympathise with that fact.

Rowan imagined himself on the stand, eyes glistening

with tears as he recounted the *awful* tragedy. He'd get the jury on side, the judge on side, and if he brought out his most charismatic self on the day, maybe even the defence lawyer. Such is the pull of a man with alpha energy.

Contemplating all of this in barely a few seconds, he dipped his lights and hit the accelerator. He didn't want to damage the vehicle too much, so he had to avoid any cars or similar obstacles that might present themselves near the figure. But the anticipation of rolling over the stranger with a guttural splat was almost too good to imagine. The risk of being caught was heavily outweighed by the voice in his head, screaming at him to do it with a maniacal cackle. Whether he liked it or not, bloodspill was his biggest lust. He'd kept it caged like an exotic animal for almost a decade, playing the good husband, the husband that accompanies his wife to every social event and every dinner with her dreadful friends. He'd swallowed every mean word, every observation, suffocated his subconscious desires until they were lifeless and swallowed up.

But today, Rowan was a changed man. The truck veered slightly left, but he quickly corrected, maintaining a direct line of travel. The silhouette—male, from what he could see in the blurry darkness—stood looking at the vehicle, his body crooked and gaze searching. Was this guy crazy? He'd had a good number of seconds to sprint out of Rowan's path now, but he was locked in place, unwilling and unmoving.

He must want to die. I'm doing a service for him. I have to do this.

The only clarity came from the deep, booming voice in his head, the one that had belonged to his Father so many years ago, before Rowan squeezed his chubby, wife-beating throat until the light in his eyes faded out.

Right now, that voice spoke only three words, rising above the mess of thoughts in his head.

"Take him out."

Yes, sir.

The gap closed quickly, and before Rowan knew it, the man slammed against the front and disappeared under the wheels. The truck vibrated as the sack of bones and flesh slowly came undone beneath the tyres, popping and disintegrating in a melody of sweet gore. It was over too quickly, and Rowan desperately searched the rearview for any evidence of his crime. Not because he was concerned, but to see his prize. There was a delightful red streak trailing a few metres behind him, but the whole scene quickly disappeared.

A spray of blood was splattered across the bonnet and windscreen, so Rowan calmly pulled a lever on the dashboard, jetting a mist of wiper fluid to clean the gristle away. His face was pulled into a wide smile, pure euphoria surging in his core. He wanted to scream, celebrate, and bottle up this feeling into a rare elixir.

He knew from experience that the only way to keep this feeling alive and burning was to kill again. Nothing could ever measure up to the feeling of the first time, but God this came close.

Right ahead, an ensemble of flashing lights signalled some kind of closure. He was low on petrol and absolutely had to make his first stop in Egglemore to refuel. By the size of the blockade of vehicles in the distance, the whole junction had been cut off, so he quickly killed his headlights and swerved to take the next turning off the motorway.

Beaverbrook Lane was not well equipped to handle heavy goods vehicles. The tight country lane only seemed to get narrower as you journeyed down it, and the corners were incredibly difficult to navigate. But judging by the flurry of activity on the motorway, he would have either been turned around or held up for a while, neither of which helped him reach his quarterly bonus for making time on his jobs.

The gentle rumble of the vehicle felt out of place amongst the silent stirring of birds and wildlife, but a low tungsten light in the distance signalled the back entrance of Timeout Central. This road was normally used by small service vehicles or residents of the cottages tucked away deep in the forest, but Rowan knew the area like the back of his hand. He'd often use the shortcut in heavy traffic to get ahead of the other HGVs and avoid queueing through his lunch breaks.

Rowan drifted through the side road, carefully calculating the scene in front of him. The blockade extended from the front entrance around the bulk of the parking lot, cutting off the entrance to the building and motel. Any chance he had of keeping hidden was rumbled almost immediately as a police officer spotted the movement.

He raised his hand and Rowan switched on his headlights, dazzling the man. He clutched his eyes with the crease of his elbow, waving his other hand in frustration. Rowan considered making a dash for it, but without fuel, there was every likelihood he wouldn't make the next stop.

"Switch off your engine and get out of the truck!" the policeman ordered in a thick Yorkshire accent. Rowan considered the command for a moment, before switching off the engine and jumping out the vehicle.

"Keys, now!" The policeman must have barely been twenty, and here he was talking to Rowan like a piece of shit. In the background, a group of officers were holding down the exits whilst a smaller team of medical staff were buzzing about in hazmat suits, cleaning the area with some kind of pressurised gas.

"What's going on?" Rowan asked, before the officer snatched his keys from him.

"You need to get inside." The officer looked at one of his colleagues and made some kind of gesture, calling them over.

"I can't stop here. I'm on a job. I'm just looking to refuel then I'll be on my way."

"Not towards Egglemore you won't. And now you're

here, I'm afraid we can't let you go back beyond the checkpoint."

"Can't let me?" Rowan snarled. As if they had a choice. He was twice their age, twice their size, and could crush mouthy little twats like them with no effort at all. But his curiosity was piqued, and whatever was going down was probably well worth getting out of the way of. Reluctantly, he followed the officer a few paces, before an almighty *smash* exploded from his right side.

The front entrance of the small, rackety motel was locked shut, the sliding doors bolted with some kind of mechanism. A group of people were trapped on the other side, beating on the glass desperately.

"What's going on?" Rowan asked, but the officers had already fled to the building. They weren't doing anything exceptionally helpful, just holding their bodies against the doors.

"Permission to shoot," one of the other officers cackled right by him. "Sir, do we have permission to shoot?"

The doors shook in their limp frames, the mechanism fighting to hold them shut. But it was no match to the over-whelming weight of a dozen bodies, eventually shattering into a spider web pattern.

"SIR?!"

Bodies spilled through the fragmented glass. They imme-diately got to their feet and began sprinting in different direc-tions, moving with ferocious determination. An old man leapt onto a female officer, wrapping his arms and legs around her body like a small monkey. His mouth plunged into her face and he ripped her nose off with very little effort, chewing on the severed flesh like a piece of taffy.

A bullet ricocheted off the metal doorframe, bouncing with a light spark. One of the armed officers paced forwards, squeezing his trigger in a calculated yet strangely frantic fash-ion. None of the bullets were making contact.

"We don't have our orders!" another officer screamed.

"Fuck orders!"

He eventually landed a hit, tearing apart one of the deranged stranger's faces. They fell with a limp thud, forehead slapping on the pavement.

Rowan was strangely elated by all the chaos. But he needed his keys. The officer that took them was on the floor, being mauled by some woman.

With no plan and a body surging with adrenaline, he dashed towards the services building. One of the mad pack tried to grab hold of him, but he effortlessly deflected the attack, sending them to the concrete. The first door he saw, a fire exit, was almost within reach.

He swept up his keys, which had spilled from the officer's grip, leaving him to be consumed by his aggressor.

Bullets sprayed, slamming into brickwork and asphalt as he sprinted. The hazmats were trying to spray the motel guests with the mystery gas, but that was doing fuck all aside from winding them up even more. Carnage unfolded, a haze of limbs and strobing gunfire.

One of the officers was half-heartedly guarding the exit whilst surveying the chaos. Rowan pushed him aside and grabbed the handle, twisting it hard. The heavy metal door swung open, revealing a pair of disorientated elderly folk and a girl who could have been pulled straight from his dreams.

CHAPTER 19
MAGGIE

The door was splintered and worn, but still wouldn't budge. Maggie had swung a metal stool at it countless times, wearing herself out in the process, but she needed a change of tack. It was physically locked, which ruled out opening it remotely.

It was God knew what time in the early hours and she'd already thought of four ways to sue these bastards. This wasn't the way lockdown procedures were meant to be implemented. She spent years working on the system herself.

She looked around the room, searching for anything that might help her get out—either through the door or by any other means possible. Her gaze settled on the ceiling.

"Wait," she said aloud. "Look there."

"What?" Claire asked.

Maggie rifled through her pocket. She kept a refillable purple lighter in her jacket alongside a single cigarette. It was a habit of sorts, a remnant of her smoking days. A comforting reminder that she was in control of her life and actions. If Maggie really wanted to smoke, she could. It was all a question of the life she wanted to lead, the kind of role model she wanted to be for her daughter.

But she wasn't planning on a cigarette break.

She sparked a flame and raised the lighter toward the ceiling.

"Ss-stopppp."

Maggie and Claire turned in unison, staring at a small nook between the back wall and a desk. Two narrow beams jutted out from behind the chair. On closer inspection, they weren't beams at all. They were legs, stockings pulled up with one shoe still clinging to a heel. Maggie let the lighter go out.

With a thunderous crack, a dishevelled woman snapped up, overextending so her chest was almost on the floor in front of her. She had a name badge dangling from her shirt, faded ink suggesting she'd done quite the stint in this office.

Her hair spilled over her face in messy strands, but her sickly eyes were staring right into Maggie's.

The woman sprawled across the floor, limbs out of place. A guttural howl bawled from her throat, distorted and wet. Despite the danger, Maggie's focus was drawn to the woman's eyes. Fearful and lost, contradicting her primal expression.

"Hey! In here!" Maggie screamed to the crowd out in the hallway. Before she could turn back, the office worker was on her feet, squatting in some kind of defensive stance. Her shoulders drove forwards, legs fast behind. Arms outstretched, the woman scuttled towards Claire with a predatory snarl.

"Claire!"

Maggie snatched a fire extinguisher from the wall and directed the nozzle at the crazed bitch. A plume of white smoke erupted from the canister, drowning her in a chalky dust. The woman crashed to the floor, flailing, grasping at anything within reach.

"Get back!"

A crooked hand wrapped around Claire's ankle, slender

fingers gripping impossibly tight. Without a second thought, Maggie drove the fire extinguisher down into the woman's arm, shattering the bone. The heavy metal reverberated against the linoleum floor, crushing right through the sinew.

The white powder from the extinguisher settled in the air, eventually triggering the fire alarm.

Sirens blared. Light echoed through the room in deep red waves, illuminating the rain-splattered windows. Maggie's heart swelled in her chest, primal instincts rising to the surface. Finally, a rattle of keys against the door.

"We need to evacuate!" an unknown voice ordered.

Maggie scooped Claire up, throwing her into the arms of the man who unlocked the door. Not willing to take any more risks, she swept back towards the office worker and booted her in the jaw.

"Claire, get here!" Maggie ordered, snatching her back from the random man. Arm tucked tightly around her daughter's shoulders, she fell back behind the crowd this time, hoping to buy some time to think. The exits were locked down. Darkness loomed beyond the maze of stark hallways, and it was impossible to predict what was going on outside the premises.

The hallway to the left passed in a blur, but Maggie froze the snapshot in her mind: a body splayed open; ropes of intestines untangled on the floor; an impossible spray of blood.

FOCUS.

Panic surged through the crowd, splitting them into pockets of frantic energy. People stopped to twist door handles, pull alarms, anything that felt minutely useful in the rush to freedom.

Breathless and overwrought, Maggie joined in, hopelessly rattling through anything she could think to try.

Bodies were forcing their way around a static silhouette.

Another faceless stranger, completely unmoving, stuck facing the rush of the crowd.

Didn't they know the exit was the other way?

Faces and torsos suffocated Maggie's view, lurching forward at a painfully slow pace. Worse still, the stranger in the middle of the crowd had an eerily similar expression to the woman in the office. The same milky eyes and snarling lips edged closer, just metres away. A teenage nightmare; youthful beauty tainted by diseased rage. The kind of girl you see at the bar, still dressed in something from a night out. Pure disgust seethed from her pores. Maggie felt a chill in her core.

Something changed in the air, and suddenly the girl's gaze fell upon an elderly gentleman in an ugly patterned night-gown, dragging an IV on its stand. She tore his throat out, feral jaws closing on lacerated flesh. Maggie squeezed her eyes shut, willing this nightmare away, but it continued to erupt around her in hyper-vibrant colour. For a moment, she wasn't sure if she was screaming or not.

Then her gaze fell upon Claire, who was standing deathly still, hands clutched to her ears. Tears cascaded from her daughter's eyes, but this wasn't a response to the violence. This was something else.

Her lips were mouthing the same words over and over again.

"I can't hear! I can't hear!"

Maggie sifted through the crowd, scraping past odour-stained armpits and sweaty back stains. The heating was full blast, stale air cycling in any space it could muster. The group hurtled to a standstill as the teenager carved flesh with her teeth and fingernails, shredding apart anyone in her way. When enough bodies had fallen, writhing with gushing wounds, the girl broke through and hurled herself into a wall, as if the structure might have let her pass through. By the time she collapsed onto the floor, people had started to pile up on her in a half-hearted attempt to crush her into submission. Instead, she blurted out a vomit of nonsense, voice crackling in a mangled pitch.

The walls were closing in, dizzying motion putting her off balance. Maggie had to get out of this fucking hallway. The final door on the left opened right up, and Maggie ensured she and Claire were the first through. Away from that animal outside, a whole host of obstacles were opening up in front of them. Stray trolleys forced the rabble of strangers into a funnel as they tripped over fresh corpses and piled into any gap that presented itself. Threads of flesh marred the walls; blood-soaked remains adhered to peeling information boards. The depths of Hell were bleeding through to this reality, a nightmarish episode on repeat, where only the lucky ones escaped with all their limbs intact.

Maggie couldn't afford to lose her mind.

And she definitely couldn't pay attention to the memory that fought so tirelessly to get her attention.

The one that tied her to this place.

Her Uncle's head, crushed against a metal fence, squeezed within an inch of his life.

"GET BACK!" a deep voice boomed.

They had finally fought their way back to the main lobby. A blinding lineup of searing torch beams cut across the space, silhouettes of weapons bobbing in plunging shadows. The main lights were out, fluorescent bulbs sputtering on and off intermittently.

Maggie couldn't tell if it was the police or the army, but her chances of getting out of this place were dwindling with every wasted minute.

"There's something behind us!" Maggie screamed towards the shadows.

"Get back in that hallway right now!" another silhouette ordered.

Maggie held up her hands, but kept inching forwards.

"Please let us out!" she said, a forceful undertone to her words. Then, the rush of the crowd knocked her forwards, overflowing from the tight doorway. Maggie fell to the floor, dragging Claire down with her. The pop of gunfire soon followed, bringing the group to a squatting position, hands covering their faces.

Guns were raised, ready to shoot. The warning fire had done its job. Who would be the first to test these limits?

One of the gunmen stepped forward, the glitching light above him revealing clues to his identity.

Soldiers. Why the fuck are soldiers here for a lockdown?

Things had gotten out of control. But the army?

Several of the lineup stepped into the light, using their weapons to split the crowd, ushering them into tighter groups.

"Everyone from *here* to *here*, with me."

A hand crunched on Maggie's shoulder, heaving her up to her feet. The soldier pushed her towards the leftmost wall to join a rabble of faceless bodies. Scattered spots of light gave only the lightest of detail to the strangers.

"Now everyone on *that* side against the opposite wall."

Claire.

Maggie pushed off the wall, heading for the other side.

"My daughter's over there, I need to—"

One of the soldiers blocked her way, grabbing her arm hard.

"Back where you were!"

Maggie fought back, stopping only when the soldier raised his gun, the barrel close enough to touch her face. She could hear Claire screaming for her, amongst the cut-off words and panicked shrieks filling the air.

"Back where you were," the soldier repeated, in a deeper, more ominous tone. Maggie hacked and spat on his face, her saliva splattering against his face guard. He shoved her back in response, launching her on her backside.

Maggie stewed in her anger for a moment, then withdrew, retreating back to the wall. Her eyes were locked on that soldier. She couldn't see much, but she'd remember exactly who he was.

"Escort them to the wards," he ordered, turning back to the lineup. Maggie wished she had his weapon. She envisioned lining him up in her sights, firing off several rounds into his back when he was least expecting it.

The various groups were in motion now, forced through doors on opposite sides of the reception area. Maggie tried to call Claire's mobile phone, clinging to her device at waist level to avoid any suspicion.

The network was out. No WIFI. No 5g. No bars.

This shit was so much worse than Maggie had expected. And now she was split from Claire, too.

She'd do whatever it took to get her back safe.

A new plan was already forming in her head.

CHAPTER 20

TODD

Todd propped Benjamin's unconscious body a few doors down from the flat, the best he and Tanya could do in their flustered states. He didn't want him to wake up and attack his Gran again, so this would at least buy them some time.

"Where are we going?" the girl asked. She was more beautiful than he could have imagined from the drone footage.

"He bit my Gran," Todd croaked. "I need to find someone to help."

"*Bit* her?" Tanya asked. "What the fuck?"

Todd headed to the stairwell. Almost immediately, he seized up with fear, sweat trickling down his back and armpits. Without the drone to scope out the area, he was running blind. It would take a few minutes to get to ground level, but the possibility of running into something on the way was enough to freeze his blood.

"Come on then, let's go," Tanya said.

"One moment," Todd swallowed, his words near silent.

"Are you okay? Did he hurt you too?"

Todd shook his head. His skull pulsated, a headache sprouting from somewhere in his brain. He knew the feeling all too well, and tried counting himself out of it, using any of the hundreds of coping strategies his therapist had taught him. It wasn't working.

His hands tingled, heartbeat erupting in a frantic dance. Reality was threatening to slip away, blurring and stirring in trails of movement and light.

"Todd. We have to go."

Todd looked at her face, which glistened with sweat and a light mist of blood. Her brow furrowed, painted with concern.

You have to snap out of this Todd.

Four things you can see.

Three things you can hear.

Someone was at the other end of the balcony. They weren't there to say hello.

Bare feet slapped against concrete slabs. A disoriented twenty-something in a torn dressing gown, wearing only boxers underneath, flailed against the balcony, catching himself in time to push back off.

"We really need to go, Todd!"

Todd took a deep breath and bolted towards the stairwell, Tanya just a few steps behind him. A gurgled howl reverberated from the building walls, leaking out into the courtyard. The dim tungsten lamps provided very little light, drowning the stairwell in darkness. Todd and Tanya manoeuvred through the narrow space, using their hands to guide them around the corners.

The winding stairs felt everlasting, a deathly descent into the unknown. Tanya toggled on the torch on her phone, blasting white light through the abyss. They passed the second floor, ready to bolt as soon as they got to ground level.

Then the strained vocalisations from behind them grew in volume, getting closer at an impossible speed.

Todd looked up, just in time to sidestep the plummeting teenager, who must have jumped from the third floor. His body crumpled into the concrete stairs, folding in on itself like a flesh accordion. A spew of putrid remains deflected off the floor, splattering over Todd's back.

The smell was unimaginable, a foul stew of body odour and expired meat. Todd gagged, but kept on moving, sprinting towards the world outside.

"Help us please!" he screamed, roaming headfirst into a carnage of chaos. The fireman from earlier was being scooped up from the top of the truck, his remains sloppy and slick. There were at least three other bodies on the floor.

A paramedic spotted them, hesitantly jogging over with a concerned look on her face.

"You need to get back inside."

"My Gran, she… Someone bit her."

The look of concern grew more pronounced.

"Bit her? Where is she now?"

"In my flat… And there are others, on the stairwell—"

"Listen to me carefully," the woman stressed. "How long ago was she bitten? Is she showing any signs?"

"Of what?" Todd asked.

"Of *this*." She gestured towards a woman strapped into a stretcher, just over by the planters. She was writhing, mangled and vomit-stained. She had the same weird eyes as the others he'd seen.

"No, she… No."

Todd looked to the floor, putting everything together in his head. Benjamin had caught something, and probably given it to his Gran. Would she fall into this rage as well?

"You and your friend need to grab your essentials and get out of this city."

"I can't leave her, she needs a doctor."

"There's nothing anyone can do. Trust me…"

"I won't abandon her," Todd said unwaveringly. "She's my family!"

The paramedic shrugged hopelessly.

"You'll wish you did."

The paramedic jogged back to her initial place, and Todd was back at square one, completely clueless and afraid.

"Someone will help," Tanya said gently. "We just need to find a proper doctor. We must know someone on the estate."

Todd couldn't concentrate on her words. A static buzzing rang in his ears. Adrenaline bubbled in his veins, but so did anger. Anger directed at that paramedic for being so dismissive. Anger at himself for being so fucking scared of everything. He was twenty-five years old, a fully grown man, and he'd left his own Grandmother to bleed out in her bed.

That's not who he wanted to be. That's not who he was.

He was going to find a way to help her.

"We need to get back up there," Todd said, directing Tanya towards the stairwell. He quickly scoped it out, checking the stairs for any sign of life. The teenager's flesh was mashed into the ground, still fresh and wet. They both slipped round the gore and paced back up to the first level, hiding in a small nook.

"I don't think I know any doctors," Todd sighed. "Do you?"

Tanya nodded, but her face wasn't as certain as her gesture. "Mrs Appelton in 544."

"544?" Todd asked. "Then let's go."

"It's next door to that guy."

Tanya nodded back over towards balcony man, who was still darting from one end to the other, trying to break down doors and wreak havoc.

"Shit."

"Yep."

The pair of them scouted the area for anything they could potentially use as a weapon. They could have swung by his flat and picked up a baseball bat or something, but he had promised his Gran he'd return with help. And to be honest, he was petrified of what he might find when he stepped back into the house. Would his Gran greet him with some offensive joke and tell him to put the kettle on, as she had the whole time they'd lived together?

Or would she be on her feet, deformed and aggressive, blinded by a seething hatred for her own Grandson?

Todd couldn't ruminate on that thought for long.

They managed to find a length of copper pipe and a discarded police baton, one of the extendable metal types. Tanya expressed interest in having the pipe, for some unknown reason, so Todd grabbed the baton.

The thought of using it on the man—or on anyone—never crossed his mind. It was better to be prepared and use it to warn him, rather than get caught short with nothing to protect themselves with. Todd clambered up the final stairwell leading onto the fifth floor and readied himself to turn the corner.

Looking just past the wall, Todd saw the businessman staring into one of the apartment windows. He gripped the baton tightly, wary of his limitations. He'd never been in a fight, let alone struck someone with a weapon. There was every chance he'd freeze up faced with a real confrontation.

Inching forwards, Todd noticed several doors hanging ajar. His gut squirmed with foreboding before his mind even noticed anything was amiss.

The front of flats 544 and 546 were strewn with blood, both torn open and ripped apart inside. Bits of Mrs Appleton were spread across the threshold between her kitchen and hallway.

"Fucking Hell!" Todd screamed, accidentally rousing the businessman.

The man lurched towards the pair, his tattered suit blowing in the freezing wind. He slammed his gaunt frame into Todd and wrapped his hands around his neck in tight coils.

Todd felt the pressure, intense and direct, his Adam's apple compressing under the force. As glittering static started to appear in his vision, a disquieting peace overcoming his body. A transcendent calm, even face-to-face with this violent monster.

Smash.

Tanya drove the copper pipe down into the man's head and his grip loosened immediately. Another swipe followed, shattering his skull and sending him down in a crumple.

"She's dead," Todd cried. "Mrs Appleton…"

"We'll find someone. Your Gran will be—"

"Heeeeeeeerrrrrggg!"

Back on his feet, the businessman plunged into Tanya, launching her into the balcony wall. His face was split into dripping segments, bone fragments jutting through the skin. Grappling with thrashing limbs, Tanya fought to break his grip, but his fervent bloodlust was inescapable. With sharp force, the businessman snatched her face to the side, pinching her flesh. Sickly delight lit up his face as he gorged on her cheek, chowing down on glossy fresh meat, slurping it up like ramen.

Todd swung the baton directly into the side of his head. The metal collided with a wet slap, shattering whatever bone was there. But it wasn't enough. With a hysterical cackle, the man grabbed Tanya and pulled her back a few feet. With his eyes fixed on the dark abyss below the balcony, he forced them both over the guardrail, handing over the reins to gravity.

Tanya bellowed, her face scrunched in fear of what she knew was coming. Her blonde hair flapped in the breeze for a moment as her outline was swallowed by shadows—before crashing into a mangled heap. Todd stopped, breathless and defeated. He was still holding the baton mid-air, in the position he'd made contact with the man. Blood trickled from the end, splashing in small drips on the concrete walkway.

"Okay… Okay… FUCK!."

Todd started running, trying to outpace the wave of

anxiety threatening to wash up and discard him in the ocean of death below. Before he knew it, he was outside his flat. His Gran was stalking in the kitchen, staring at the kettle as though it might grow arms and make the tea itself. Todd's heart ached, his chest constricting and threatening to cut off his entire blood supply.

There was nothing behind her eyes. He'd only caught a glance, but the bubbly cockney charm had dissipated, a shell of a woman masquerading as his Gran. In that moment, she looked oddly at ease, in her own bubble with none of the baggage of the life she knew an hour ago. He stared for as long as he could, burning her image into his mind.

Get your shit and go. Go.

Todd couldn't confront the woman in the kitchen. He couldn't see those eyes up close.

His bedroom window faced right out onto the balcony, and it was still propped open from when he'd recalled the drone. With clumsy vigour, he pulled the mechanism as wide as it would go and propped his leg over the frame. His foot crashed into a neat stack of books on the windowsill, knocking them to the floor.

Todd paused for a moment, trying to slow his breathing. His focus was on the door dividing his room and the kitchen.

He couldn't let her see him. He couldn't see those eyes.

Balance restored, he was inside, desperately searching for a bag. Silently lamenting his choice of style over practicality, he finally uncovered a grey duffel bag, and the specialty backpack his drone and controls were packed into. He shook the miscellaneous items from inside the pockets and set his sights on essentials.

Clothes. Money. Passport? What the fuck do I take?

Todd could hear something. An undulating mutter, nonsense manifesting in patterns.

It was coming from the kitchen.

Fuck fuck fuck.

He grabbed handfuls of stuff, desperately hoping his subconscious was directing him in some way. There was a bit of change on the side; his credit card and passport were in a sleeve. That all went in the duffle bag, followed by a tangle of clothes and half-used toiletries.

The handle on his door rattled.

He quickly grabbed his phone, scooped up the drone and controls, and edged towards the window. Quickly wrapping a raincoat around him, Todd looked back at his bedroom for a final time.

The door handle rattled again. Then it made a full rotation.

Give me ten seconds to get out. Please God, don't make me look at her.

The door crept open, revealing his Gran in stark silhouette, the kitchen fluorescents backlighting her slender frame. The distant hum of the refrigerator vibrated through the apartment, audible only in terrifying silences like this one.

Todd swallowed, gripping the window frame with his right hand. His body was still faced towards his Gran, open and unthreatening. He didn't want to make a wrong move. Edging ever closer to the outdoors, he held his breath, his throat raw with emotion and unspoken words.

"Heeeeellllppp," she croaked, her syllables a long, distorted drawl. Her wound was tinged a sickly purple, exposed by an upturned table lamp discarded on the floor. Locked in a standstill, it was up to one of them to make a first move.

Todd decided it had to be him.

He made a beeline for the window, leaping at twice his usual pace in an effort to outrun her. Todd knew the speed she usually moved at, but he'd also seen Benjamin launch himself halfway across the kitchen and get back on his feet within a split second. The old rules didn't apply.

Proving his theory, his Gran was at the window by the

time his leg dangled onto the balcony. She grabbed his shirt, tearing him back towards the room, his own personal sanctuary forever marred by the day's events. Todd tried to force her fingers from his clothes, but her grip was titanium.

"Let go, Gran! Please!"

He tried to shake her away, get enough momentum to swing his body out onto the balcony, but she was relentless. Todd's fingers brushed against one of the hardback books still leant on the windowsill, and he quickly placed the spine against her gnashing mouth.

He slammed the heel of his other hand into the book, forcing her head backwards with a stomach-turning crack. Repositioning himself to swing out onto the balcony, he fumbled to grab the baton, which had fallen onto the desk right by the wall.

His Gran mumbled some kind of colourful vitriol and made another run at him. He closed his eyes and extended the tip of the baton in her direction, silently willing the whole thing to be over in one way or another. He was too exhausted to keep fighting.

Moments later, he felt a pop and a slurry of sticky broth trickle down onto his fingers.

The world came back to him in slow streaks as he slowly allowed his eyelids to open. His Gran was inches away, face contorted in silent horror. The baton had punctured her eye, and ripped through until it reached her skull. He could feel the muscle slick around the metal with every laboured breath she took.

Todd retracted the baton in one quick swipe, ripping out bits of brain and the last remnants of life from the elderly woman. She fell back dramatically, thudding to the carpet. Todd remained halfway in and out of the window for several minutes, feeling his body rise and fall with strained breaths.

His mind locked on the scene in front of him. Parts of his Gran were in his room. The flesh from her shin was split between the kitchen and Benjamin's teeth. Some of her was on his baton.

The vomiting came quickly, spewing from his lips in a heavy torrent.

He couldn't leave her like that.

Todd slinked into the kitchen and found the pile of tea towels from the cupboard. Trails of sticky blood ran in patterns across the floor and furniture, staining just about everything in some way or another. Todd sifted through the pile of towels on the table, and found his Gran's prized possession: a Platinum Jubilee towel from 2022, adorned with fancy graphics and a big picture of the Queen's face. The former monarch stared out from the fabric, her face apathetic and unbothered.

Back in the bedroom, Todd draped the towel over her face, letting it flop back gently onto her hair.

Eventually, he stepped out onto the balcony, legs shaking, arms exhausted and trailing by his sides. The baton hung limply between his fingers, the lives of two people weighing heavy on the weapon.

Benjamin had disappeared. Todd almost didn't notice.

With a final, lingering glance at his Gran, Todd turned his back against the window and started to weep. He swept up his bags and picked a direction, sprinting until he was far from the estate and the menagerie of murder and mayhem unravelling in those walls.

Half a mile down the road, there was a park thick with towering trees and dense foliage. He'd scoped it out plenty of times with the drone, and with a few hours until daylight, it was imperative he found somewhere safe to rest.

Todd only stopped running when the light was choked from every space around him under the cover of the majestic oaks. A small, brick shelter was nestled into the corner of a winding path, a public toilet by the looks of it. Todd shone his torch on the door, read the sign, and tried the lock. Thankfully, it twisted open, revealing a tiny, tiled bathroom, with two urinals and one cubicle.

Teetering on the edge, Todd pushed through to the cubicle and collapsed onto the toilet lid. From his bag, he pulled out a couple of jumpers and threw them on over his jacket, densely packed out like some kind of spacesuit.

The air went heavy and his eyelids drifted together slowly. With his head resting against the cold wall, he slept for hours.

DAY 2

CHAPTER 21
CHARLES

Something was very wrong with this place.

He'd seen it in the raincoat guy at the gym and suspected a similar thing was happening with his tent-neighbour Janine yesterday. Was it another pandemic? Some kind of bug?

Charles was used to feeling vulnerable on the cold city streets, but the feeling he had right now was unmistakable. A sheer discomfort, an awareness that this city could swallow the entire population whole with no mercy.

Sunrise was breaking through above, but the city was anything but peaceful. Distant sirens and haunting, broken screams danced in the air, with short bursts of silence the only respite from the chaos.

Charles was making his way back to the town centre. His exact plan was still brewing in his mind, but he could potentially take a shortcut back to the underpass and pack up his tent, ready to move somewhere safer. Maybe he could hit up Rod and see if the offer of staying in the shop still stood. Something told him things were about to get much worse before they got better, so moving to an area less populated was a priority.

As he walked, the pain in Charles' shoulder was painfully

tender, every movement complete agony. He tried to balance the messenger bag on his left shoulder, but it put him off balance, an unusual and foreign feeling after such an ingrained habit. Instead, he twisted the strap to have the bag settle on his lower back instead, removing some of the weight.

At every corner, Charles was hyper-aware, his mind hunting for any unusual movement or sounds. A police car dashed out of a junction, speeding towards something with little regard to its surroundings. A sense of urgency emanated from every vehicle, every stranger. Things were spiralling, but with no explanation as to how or why. Not yet, at least.

After another ten minutes of walking, Charles gathered some of the change rattling around in the bottom of his bag, and hopped into a nondescript café. An old LCD television was hung in the corner of the cramped space, intermittently glitching with wavy static. The whole place was pretty run down, but he wanted to watch the news, which always seemed to be on a loop here. Plus, he could get a coffee for less than £1.50, which was unheard of anywhere in the city. It wasn't the best, but it would perk him up and give him some time to catch up on events.

A young, female newsreader stared into the camera on-screen, reeling off local news before stopping for a few moments.

"Breaking news coming in from Egglemore. The government has announced a city-wide curfew from 12:00pm. All residents are to return home by 12:00pm, and stay inside until further notice. This measure follows an emergency alert in the late hours of last night, which was delivered to mobile devices."

Charles rolled his eyes, grabbing his styrofoam cup of coffee from the counter. He didn't have a home to return to let alone a mobile phone to receive emergency alerts. The government had a way of forgetting anyone that didn't fit neatly into their preconceived notions of society, and though he didn't let it affect him day to day, it was situations like this that really drove their ignorance home.

He took a sip of his coffee, and resolved to take a breather to give himself a moment to think. There were only two other customers in the shop, over in the far corner, and they were keeping to themselves. They didn't seem to react to the news at all, aside from a couple of snide remarks.

"Trying to keep us indoors again are they? What are they up to this time?"

"It's all a conspiracy. Just gangs and drugs and shit."

Charles looked back at the TV.

"An increased police presence will be introduced in light of a wave of violence in pockets of the city," the newsreader continued. "If you have any questions, please visit the Egglemore Council website, or call 101."

Not a moment after the newsreader finished her sentence, a convoy of five or six black vehicles sped past the café. The windows were tinted, license plates blacked out. Charles rushed up, grabbed his belongings, and made it out in time to see the vehicles fan out in three different directions, two cars down each main road. They were the exact same models that he'd seen the day before.

"Do you know who they are?" he asked the waitress, running back into the café. She shook her head apathetically, offering little more than a grunt.

Charles thanked her and went on his way. He couldn't help but feel anxious after the run-in at the gym, but he wasn't going to spiral. Instead, he'd get his things and head to Ravensbrook Park, a huge forest about two miles north of the underpass. He'd have time to think there. To plan. He couldn't spend another second delaying—he had to go.

The bright sound of noughties pop brought some peace back to his reality. Charles had the volume up high, walking in beat with the music, ignoring the red-hot pleading of his shoulder and any weird sounds that might have otherwise stopped him in his tracks.

He broke down his pop-up tent and grabbed a bag full of his belongings at the underpass, and was now on the outskirts of the park. Rows of apartments ran along the perimeter, multi-level structures adorned with opulent Georgian façades and ornate detailing. From the entrance, he could see lines of balconies overlooking the acres of forest, but no-one out enjoying the view. It was a shame so many of the houses were empty for ten out of twelve months, second homes for those with the luxury to afford them. If he had one of those places, he'd be out drinking cocktails on the balcony every day.

Stranger things have happened.

A droplet of water dripped onto Charles' head, sinking deep in his scalp. Seconds later, the heavens opened, and he found himself hiding under a massive oak tree, clumsily positioning himself to get as much cover as possible. He had a foldable mac raincoat in his bag, but getting it wet now would mean no protection for later. And with the weather as unpredictable as it had been lately, he needed to be wary of his resources.

A heavy wind swept up out of nowhere, causing the branches to sway and tangle overhead. The skies were angry, stained a deep blue. The chill cut through every layer Charles was wearing, making his skin prickle with goosebumps. The tree was offering no protection now, so he took a deep breath and made a run for it, desperately searching for more cover. In every direction, there was nothing but grass and foliage. It might have been a mistake leaving the underpass after all…

"GET THE FUCK OFF OF ME!"

It was a woman's voice, young and petrified. The words

echoed around the park, bouncing from tree to tree. Charles stopped moving, trying to discern what direction it came from.

"SOMEONE HELP!"

The apartments.

Charles ran towards the back gates of the buildings, searching for a shortcut through to the front. They were securely locked, and there was no public route back to the road, so he sprinted around the long way. By chance, he happened upon one of the black vehicles parked outside. Two men in suits were wrestling to get a girl in the car. Dirty pastel pink hair, heavy makeup, torn jeans. Not the kind of person Charles would expect to live in one of these houses, but he knew better than to make judgements based on looks alone. He'd been very fortunate that people had given him the same treatment when they first met him.

"Hey!" he shouted, running over to the car. "Leave her alone!"

The girl spotted Charles and it seemed to give her a second wind to keep fighting them off. Planting her feet in the tarmac, she swung her arm and elbowed one of the suits, before kneeing the other in the nuts. One of them tried to punch her back, but slipped on the wet pavement, smashing the back of his head into the car. Charles jumped in front of the woman, protecting her with his body. He raised his hands, trying to de-escalate the situation.

"Leave her!" one of the men called out. "We need to get the next one."

They jumped into the car and quickly sped off, disappearing over the horizon.

The girl backtracked towards her house and gestured for Charles to follow. He jogged over to join her inside.

"What was that all about?" he asked, as she quickly slammed the door behind him.

"Shit," she spat, distracted by something. She scurried off

into the main living area, and Charles followed, stumbling to remove his shoes. The apartment was like nothing he'd seen before: a vast space, broken into zones by tasteful wallpaper and soft furnishings. Every inch had been considered, with plenty of chairs, table space, and a handful of expensive-looking art pieces.

Looking beneath the surface, the place did seem dustier than it should have been, and there were clothes scattered across one of the sofas. A weird swirl of smoke hung in the air near the living area, accompanied by the strong stench of weed.

The girl brushed some ash from a small side table and picked up a half-smoked joint. She lifted the tip to her lips and inhaled. She fell back onto one of the sofas and squeezed her eyes shut.

"Could have burned the apartment down if they'd taken me," she said in between tokes. "Didn't even have a chance to put it out before they got here."

Charles placed his tent and bags by a shoe rack, wincing in pain.

"You want some?" she asked, clocking his discomfort. "You look like you could do with it."

Charles shook his head politely.

"Thank you, though."

She shrugged, and took an even bigger puff herself, holding the breath before exhaling hard.

"Who were those guys?" he asked, heading towards the sofas. The girl invited him to take a seat on the adjacent one to her.

"Lackeys, I presume."

"I'm not following."

The girl took another puff, and extinguished the stub in the ashtray.

"All I know is I got a message at some stupid hour about

leaving the city," she started. "No warning, no time to wash some clothes."

Charles relaxed back on the sofa, making the most of the cloud-soft cushions and springy texture.

"Who sent the message?"

The girl shrugged again.

"The company, I guess."

She noticed Charles' eyes starting to glaze over, so offered a little more in the way of an explanation.

"My mum works at this big science company. They're getting all the families to an emergency shelter."

Charles squinted.

"A shelter?"

"Yep," she said matter-of-factly. "I'm not going though. I'm meant to be meeting someone."

"And this is to do with the curfew, right?"

The girl sighed.

"I really don't know the ins and outs. I just got back from uni two days ago. Can we have some wine instead of going over this?"

Without waiting for an answer, she jumped up and over to the fridge, grabbing a half-full bottle of rosé. She shoved a glass into Charles' hand and filled it to the top.

"Oh, thank you, I—"

The girl glugged half of her drink, then slammed it down onto the table.

"Just one more question," Charles said. "What's your name?"

The girl smiled, caught off-guard.

"I'm Olive."

Charles took a small sip of the wine. It was crisp, fruity, and dangerously drinkable. He hadn't touched alcohol in months, so he knew he'd have to take it slow. Especially given the situation.

"I'm Charles. Nice to meet you."

Olive smiled, her dark red lips curling at the edges.

"So, Charles, tell me about *you*. How old are you? Where do you live?"

Charles cleared his throat, grabbing his glass. A little more wouldn't hurt.

"Well…I'm 42. I live under a bridge, well, currently no fixed abode. I like music and those jerk chicken wings you get at the station."

"Under the bridge? Are you—"

"Homeless. I am, yes. I was hoping to set up my tent in the forest, but the weather had different ideas."

Olive shook her head.

"I was going to say a *troll* actually. You know, living under a bridge and all…"

"Oh," Charles mustered. "I'm not a troll."

"I know, silly. But you can't be out there. You'll stay here in the guest room. Until this blows over."

"I can't accept—"

She shook her head again, an over the top gesture potentially influenced by the Californian White Zinfandel.

"They've all fucked off to the shelter anyway, so there's plenty of space. I have wine, snacks, weed. Video games…"

"What's the shower like?"

Olive grinned.

"Five jets. Every angle you can imagine."

Charles mirrored her smile.

"I guess I'll stay to give that a go."

CHAPTER 22

ALICE

Alice sat opposite a towering man with slick brown hair and a lanky yet defined frame. His clothes were dusty and marred, a casual t-shirt and jeans combo suggesting he didn't work here. But she also hadn't seen him around the whole day yesterday, so where had he appeared from in the early hours?

The night had passed without any more violence, breaking into a groggy, coffee-fuelled morning full of frustration and apathy. Some people had slept on the floor, others hadn't slept at all. Alice was one of the all-nighters, staying up to talk to this guy, who had shown up at the fire exit in the middle of a gunfight.

Rowan. Rowan Matthews.

For all of his alluring mystery, his life sounded pretty standard. Job as a HGV driver. No wife or kids. Always on the road, just caught in the middle of a long night's driving. Nothing special at all.

But Alice could sense something in his eyes. The suggestion that there was something more, something he was keeping hidden.

"I was just stopping to refuel," he said, continuing a story about how he got to the service station. "Should have been a half hour stop and straight to Egglemore for the night."

"Yeah. We weren't planning on this either."

Rhys was sitting with the elderly couple at an adjacent table in the food hall. The staff had provided coffee and pastries, just enough to make a small dent in the collective hunger, but people were already asking for extra milk and more food, treating them as if they hadn't also had the bare minimum of sleep.

"So what *is* the plan?" Rowan asked expectantly, staring at Alice as though she was the leader of this group of stragglers.

"We were going to find an exit and a vehicle. Then you showed up with all that mayhem."

"That wasn't me actually," Rowan corrected. "It was a case of bad timing. Some crazy guy attacked the officers."

Alice nodded.

"Yeah, there's been a lot of that."

Rowan hadn't realised the scale of the violence, having travelled in from out of county. He'd mentioned getting to the depot and everything being fine, and seeing someone walking on the side of the motorway, but nothing concerning until the cordon at the services entrance.

Alice had explained the fights and the bloodshed, keeping the grisly details as vague as possible. Rhys didn't react to any of it, blocking out any mention of his brother or the coach journey. Even the elderly couple, who had made a habit of blurting out their feelings at the most inopportune times, were silent, giving space to Alice's recollection.

The mobile network had been out the whole night. She felt great frustration at being held up from her meeting, and the fact that her phone was already down to 30% battery meant it probably wouldn't be happening anytime soon. Hopefully the anonymous woman wouldn't change her mind about talking to Alice. She had a feeling her career hung in the balance of this story.

"Do any of you have a charger?" Alice asked the group, shifting the conversation.

They all shook their heads.

"I have one in the truck," Rowan said. "But the officers out there are pissed off, and maybe a bit trigger-happy, given the situation."

Alice nodded. "I can wait. It's no rush."

Rhys tapped his phone screen. "The network's still out anyway. We can't contact anyone."

No shit, kid. But we need to try.

"Why is no-one trying to help us?" the old woman lamented. "He's still not had any help with his head."

She gestured at her husband, who had fashioned a bandage from a t-shirt.

"I'm okay," he added. "I don't want to make any fuss."

"That boy *ripped your hair out*," the woman spat, albeit at a whisper in the presence of Rhys. Not that his eyes even shifted at the mention of his rabid brother. His eyes didn't shift at anything.

Rowan cleared his throat, ready to steer the conversation again.

"We should try and get back to the truck when it's dark," he said. "Try and surprise them."

"And get shot in the face?" the elderly woman asked. "No thank you."

Rowan straightened his back, adjusting on the hard plastic seats.

"You're welcome to stay," he said rather directly. "But I don't want to be held hostage when I'm just trying to do my job and get home."

He had a point. They had to try something.

"How far are we from the city?" Alice asked.

"A mile or two. But they've blocked all traffic in and out. I can't even go back."

"There must be other routes. Country roads or something?"

Rowan shook his head.

Alice exhaled, breathing through the stress of it all.

"Well, we can't stay. It's only a matter of time until one of those *things* get us."

Rowan nodded.

"Precisely."

"So we're storming the cordon in a HGV, *if* we make it to the truck without being shot?"

"Yep," Rowan answered. "Just after 6:00pm."

An alert rang through on their mobile phones. Hoping that this meant the network was back up, Alice tapped it. There was no signal or 5G. The emergency alert system had a way of sending messages without any of that.

She sighed, reading the message.

"Timeout Central visitors. We have locked down the site whilst we investigate a potential biological hazard. We will be issuing more information soon. Please keep calm, and make use of the facilities."

"Fucking great," Rhys groaned.

Alice excused herself and strolled over to the window. The courtyard was strewn with the odd body bag and tattered hazard tape. The exits were still being guarded by officers, who looked just as worn out as she felt. One of them even gave her a friendly, knowing stare, as if they were navigating this shitshow together. She returned the smile, then took another look around the space. Families hunched over tables, sharing the last scraps of food, trying to maintain some level of normality with chit-chat and brief flickers of laughter.

A strange metallic rattle drew her attention, just over the way. Curious, Alice tracked around to discover a steel shutter, bolted shut with a padlock. It was clattering in violent bursts, as if someone was trying to break in from the other side.

Just above the mechanism, another garish sign marked the entrance to the Timeout Motel.

Wait.

Alice jogged back over to the window and saw a narrow corridor connecting the two buildings, only wide enough for a person or two. A covered route from the complex to the motel reception.

They're joined together.

The entire motel was shuttered, so there weren't nearly as many officers watching those exterior doors. If they could find a way through, they might just stand a chance at catching the police off-guard, enough time to get to the vehicle.

Alice didn't trust this Rowan guy particularly, but he did have a truck, which would get her closer to the city if not all the way in. That's all she needed to focus on right now.

"I might have a plan," she announced to her little group back in the food hall.

She sat down, gesturing at them to lean in. The old woman rolled her eyes, before finally listening.

"There's a shutter connecting us to the motel. If we can make it through there, we might get out."

Rowan shook his head, instantly dismissing the idea.

"It's full of those people. That's what caused the fight last night."

"We have to try. Maybe we could move them, and—"

"Move them?" Rowan challenged. "They took out half a team of police officers, and you think we can just shuffle them out the way?"

Alice squinted at him, rising to the confrontation.

"You have a better idea then, in *your* plan? Should we just walk out the front door? Sure they won't expect that."

"Sorry, I don't mean it like that. It's just that motel was heaving when the first one of them escaped. Then it got crazy. I just about survived getting through that fire exit."

"They've been putting all the bodies in there," Rhys muttered, joining the conversation. "I think Jake is in there. Paramedics too."

"What?" Alice asked, turning to him.

"I've been walking around. I saw them doing it yesterday."

"So everyone in there was dead?"

Rhys shook his head.

"A few of them were just injured. But now they're all... *like that.*"

The elderly woman scowled.

"So it's spreading? To all of us? And we're here huddled in like fucking fools."

Alice shook her head assertively.

"No. Not through the air. Otherwise it would have happened already... Rhys, was Jake hurt before the coach?"

Rhys had managed to ignore any passing comments or discussions about Jake, but this question was so direct it would be impossible not to answer.

"I already said, nothing was wrong with him at all. I just..."

He trailed off, ending his part in the conversation. His eyes tracked the walls in front of him, refusing to engage.

Alice cussed under her breath, absolutely sick of it all.

"What if we let them out instead?" Rowan offered.

The elderly woman near enough broke her neck, the speed with which she recoiled.

"*Those* people? Let them in here?"

"It would be carnage," Alice said. "We could get hurt."

"We could get hurt anyway," Rowan fired back. "We'd put everyone in the far corner, make a barricade from the tables. Then one person on the shutter, one on a fire exit."

Alice's stomach stirred, already nervous at what her part would be in this plan.

"First person opens the shutter and returns to the group. Second person shouts and makes a scene to draw them over. They open the fire exit and quickly lock themselves in that janitor closet."

"So we'd be trapped?" Alice scoffed.

"We'd wait for them to funnel out, start causing a scene outside. Get all the officers on the defensive, then we run through to the motel and out the back door to the truck."

"That's impossible," the elderly man argued, piping up for the first time.

"It might not be," Alice countered, slowly coming around to the idea. "We'd have to get everyone on board."

"Leave that to me," Rowan said, beaming with some kind of misplaced confidence. Getting a busload of grouchy strangers to put their life on the line was far from an easy task.

Alice couldn't wait to get to the city and never speak to any of these people again.

CHAPTER 23
MAGGIE

"That's fucking insane. No way."

Not quite the reaction she had expected, but even Maggie had to admit her plan was drastic. Especially for this time in the morning, after a night of no sleep.

She had shared her idea with a random woman in her group once the soldiers had left them in the waiting area.

They were in a small room, light blue walls and rows of plastic white chairs with curtained-off nooks to evaluate patients. The woman next to her was young, probably early 30s, and looked to be heavily pregnant. Her partner was nowhere to be found, so they shared a determination to get back to their families. She just didn't appear to be willing to go the lengths Maggie was planning to do so.

Maggie stood up, drawing the eye of several other visitors. Their concerned gestures were almost a warning: *sit down or you'll get us all in trouble.*

But she wasn't bothered about a bit of trouble. Her only concern was getting to Claire, and that involved some creative thinking. Maggie explored the space, pulling back curtains in search of something flammable. Hand sanitiser or some kind of cleaning fluid. Rubbing alcohol would be even better.

As she leant down to search lower-level shelves and cupboards, the small plastic lighter from before bulged in her back pocket.

That lighter would come in handy again. She was planning to set a fire and force the soldiers to help them evacuate. The visitors' lives were in their hands, and they wouldn't risk the bad press of burning hundreds of people alive whilst holding them hostage.

The roller blind on the central window was locked in place, so Maggie forced it off its frame. The parking lot outside was devoid of life, just cars and a couple of army vehicles. She swiped an industrial sized bottle of hand sanitiser from one of the wash stations and decanted it into a couple of sterile glass bottles.

The rest of the group were already muttering under their breath, deciding whether to help Maggie out or stop her from making a big mistake. Whatever their opinion, she wasn't going to stop, so she tore some fabric from a divider curtain and made her own rudimentary Molotov cocktails.

"You can't be serious," the woman from the seat over called out. "You'll burn us alive."

"I'm going to drop it out the window. There's a patch of grass just there. The smoke should sift back in and set off the alarm."

"And if it spreads up the wall and creates a bigger fire outside?"

Maggie smirked.

"Then they'll have to evacuate us quicker. I can see they're watching me now."

She raised her head to the CCTV camera on the ceiling, a red light flickering under the console.

"They're probably on their way so we need to be quick," Maggie explained.

"There's no *we* in this, love," the woman spat, returning her attention to one of the free magazines.

Maggie shrugged and forced the top window open.

"Maybe think about this for a moment?" a male voice begged.

"You're a fucking lunatic," another voice added.

She set alight to the fabric poking from the top of the bottle and let the flame spread for a split second. Then she manoeuvred the bottle through the frame and let it drop to the grass outside.

A plume of flames erupted from the ground, setting alight to the overgrown grass. Some of it caught on the wall for a moment, but quickly dissipated. Maggie had already started to light the second bottle when a soldier crashed through the door.

Maggie tensed up, the loud bang making her jump. The bottle tumbled to the floor right by her, catching on the linoleum and the discarded roller blind. Before she knew it, smoke choked the air, and people were sprinting towards the exit.

"Shit!"

The table of magazines was next to go up in flames, the fire roaring in intensity. Maggie shuffled through the haze, feeling the heat emanating behind her. Sprinklers in the ceiling burst to life, drowning the area in a heavy mist. The stale water drenched through her jacket, splashing on the floor in tiny puddles.

"Move!" Maggie ordered, shoving the people in front of her. The soldier was already at the end of the hallway, sprinting for his own life. It was survival of the fittest, and Maggie was far from that. She needed to survive, nevertheless.

Smoke filled the reception, hanging thick in the air. It was hard to see a metre in front of her, let alone work out a path to Claire. The idea might have been too drastic; she should have listened to the pregnant woman. Her heart was racing with the knowledge that she'd put all these people in danger, and she silently lamented her reckless actions.

But there was no changing the past, so she charged ahead, using the torch on her phone to guide her. On her way out, she grabbed a couple of stragglers, forcing them into the crowd and out of the way of the flames. She couldn't let anyone get hurt because of her.

As she expected, the other groups started to rush from the opposite hallway. She tracked the crowd for Claire, hoping to God she'd be near the front so they could make their escape. In the middle of the first crowd, she saw her daughter, panicked but determined.

"Claire! Claire, I'm right in front of you!"

Some idiot whacked into Maggie's shoulder, driving her backwards, but she quickly found her balance. Claire jumped into her arms, her hair soaked by the sprinklers too.

"We're getting out of here. Let's go—"

A gunshot thundered mere inches from Maggie's head. The bullet splatted into someone's flesh a few feet in front of her. The cloudy daylight streaming through the skylights gave the room a flat, desaturated feel, so blindingly raw that it felt almost dreamlike. Seeing blood splattered across everyone's faces didn't detract from that uncanniness.

Claire covered her ears, screaming at the head-splitting sound of the gunshot. Maggie hugged her in close, pulling away from the trigger-happy soldier. The room was moving in slow-motion.

People screamed, falling to the floor with blood spurting from their necks.

Some of those rage-filled strangers were caught in the crowd again. Carnage was unleashed by soldiers' bullets and strangers' teeth. It was like something ripped from Maggie's worst nightmares.

If those soldiers had been sent in to save the visitors, they'd damn well failed.

How many of the victims on the floor deserved a gunshot to the head? They certainly weren't all *diseased.* There were bound to be those caught in a crossfire, which is why armed response forces didn't act like this. These soldiers were poorly trained or out for blood, or maybe a mix of both.

Which is why she desperately needed to remove herself and Claire from the situation. A situation that she wasn't blameless in creating. Not by a long shot.

A few people were already working on the doors, forcing the mechanisms and loosening hinges. No cellular service meant no access to her security app—no way for her to help on that front.

Instead, she grabbed a gun from the floor, wielding it via the barrel and swinging it towards anyone acting even slightly aggressively.

Maggie was prepared to fight with everything she had.

Even Claire was doing her bit, letting out her teenage fury in backhands and slaps, though her focus was on anyone getting in her way, not just the infected.

It was a weird term that had come to Maggie: the *infected.* There was no doubt in her mind that these people were diseased somehow, whether biologically or mentally. Something was making them act this way, and though she didn't have the knowledge to comprehend just what that might be, it was an affliction of rage, a breakdown of their personalities.

With a glorious squeak, the first set of doors were open, quickly followed by the rotating ones at the entrance. The soldiers had given up trying to control the situation, standing down from their positions and joining the crowd. A couple of them tried to stand strong and be brave, but were soon mowed down and gouged apart.

Cold air rushed across Maggie's face as soon as she was

outside, sending a chill right through her body. The wet jacket wasn't helping, but she'd escaped. They had escaped.

"Where did I park?" Maggie asked. Claire laughed, a mix of nervous energy and exhaustion. They headed towards the back of the lot, scanning the spaces for the blue Ford Focus. Vehicles were already reversing, taking out each other's headlights and wing mirrors with the delirium of freedom. Maggie grabbed her keys and finally stumbled upon the car, almost entirely by accident.

"Get in!" she directed, rushing to open the door for Claire. She jumped right into the driver's seat, and Claire was in hers a few seconds later. The engine stuttered to life. Maggie checked the mirrors for anyone in her way.

And then she froze, and sat for a moment. Her head was heavy, a sense of overwhelming guilt building in her chest. They'd escaped, but at what cost? How many lives had she put in danger? Was that really the best way out of that situation?

She couldn't think about it. Not now.

She and Claire were safe. That's all that mattered.

Maggie reversed sharply, scratching the back of the adjacent car.

She snatched the gearstick forwards and compressed the accelerator, careening towards the queue forming near the exit.

CHAPTER 24
ROWAN

He really needed this to work. Being locked in with these people was bad enough, but he also felt a pang of urgency to watch his wife, and that meant finding somewhere with signal. The idea of her laying in her own filth, slowly losing grip on reality, babbling in dehydrated gurgles, was too tanta-lising to resist. He needed that release. He needed to see her suffer.

Rowan had opted for the second role in his plan, opening the fire exit when the crazed people were let into the complex. Rhys was in charge of letting them through the shutter, but that was a disaster waiting to happen. His head was in the clouds -- something about his brother. Rowan didn't really care, but he needed him to pull his weight.

Alice was on the mezzanine level, a narrow space that housed a few tables and chairs, offering picturesque views of the capitalist nightmare below. She nodded at him, ready to get this plan in action.

Two men had helped get the padlock off the shutter, with brute force and creative use of the few tools they'd managed to gather from the building. They transferred responsibility of the barely-closed mechanism to Rhys and backed away, retreating to be with their families.

It was time to go.

"Now!" Rowan ordered, aware that his voice would probably catch the attention of the police outside. It was too late for them to do anything now.

Rhys ripped the shutter up and backed away slowly. He looked as if he was barely aware of the environment, staring at the violent stream of bodies as they contorted and shoved their way through the narrow opening. Rowan started clashing a wrench against a plastic wet floor sign, creating as much noise as possible.

"Rhys, get back!" Alice screamed. But Rhys didn't listen. Instead, he ran towards the action, into the storm of barbarity erupting from the motel. Alice looked as if she was about to go after him—Rowan didn't want that.

Rhys was already gone, on some wild goose chase to find his brother's body. Completely fucking useless, but at least he did his job before he fucked off.

"Leave him!" Rowan ordered, catching Alice's gaze. There was no way he could do this on his own, and needed as many bodies as possible to *throw under the bus*, so to speak, if push came to shove.

He immediately charged a few steps towards the chaotic surge of strangers, banging the wrench hard to get their attention. Somehow, it worked. Turning awkwardly to change direction, they spilled over each other in pursuit of the loud clanging.

Rowan sprinted around to the fire exit and slammed all of his weight into it, launching the officer on the other side to the ground.

"What the fuck?" Rowan heard the officer scream, just as he backtracked to swipe open the janitor closet. With nearly perfect timing, Rowan locked himself in the tiny space, the consuming darkness a blanket from the riot outside. With only his heavy breathing audible in the closet, he could hear every detail of the outside world: bodies colliding with the metal door, growling in stunted slurs, gunfire popping off in the near distance. The first scream probably belonged to the officer on the floor, and it didn't last long.

From what Rowan could discern, all of the sound was coming from beyond the fire exit, which was intermittently slamming open and shut, new bodies catching up to their motel kin.

That meant the plan had worked.

That meant he had to move.

Inhaling deeply, he listened out for the last of the scuttering footsteps outside the closet and slowly unlocked the door.

Rowan manoeuvred his frame out of the closet and made his way back to the main area. The civilians were all squashed behind a pile of tables, waiting in uneasy anticipation. Alice was back on the ground level, happy to see him.

"It's now or never. Come on!"

Rowan and Alice took the lead, waving over the rest of the group. In a surprisingly calm manner, they all followed in a single file line, frantic but neatly organised. Rowan didn't have any more than a vague idea on how the rest of this would pan out, but the important thing was getting to his truck. And if this Alice girl wanted to come with him, he wouldn't put up a fight.

She was feisty, stunning, and confident. The holy trinity of womanhood in his opinion, and characteristics his wife had shared in the first few years of their marriage. If Alice wanted to hang out with Rowan for a while, she had an open invitation.

Through the windows, Rowan could see the motel guests overpowering the officers, depleting their numbers with breathtaking ease. He needed some of them alive as a distraction, so hopefully they wouldn't all perish just yet.

"Hurry up!" he called to Alice, aware of the dwindling likelihood of a safe escape. He broke through the swinging doors at the other end of the corridor, entering the motel reception. It was dead, metaphorically and figuratively, with a few bodies on the ground and crumbling, worn décor.

"Rhys! Where are you?" Alice screamed. Rowan sped ahead; no time to look for stragglers. On the floor, one of the bastards looked as if he was still breathing so Rowan stamped on his head, forcing his black boot through chunks of wet skull.

He wasn't taking any chances.

"Oh fuck!" Alice recoiled. Rowan could really do without the distractions, but he followed her voice anyway, pacing over to a small office just behind the reception desk. Inside, a stew of rotten scents rushed at his face as he saw Rhys hunched on the floor, crying over a corpse with a twisted neck.

What was slightly more concerning: there was another kid sinking his teeth into Rhys's ankle, his own body splayed on the floor, no movement from the torso down. An upturned wheelchair suggested the guy had pulled himself over and simply started to chomp down.

A series of bite marks peppered Rhys's legs and back, but he was still alive. Ignorant to it all, he cried over his dead brother and the unlucky fate they both shared in this place. Rhys was hardly reacting to his flesh being torn into pieces. Probably in shock or something.

Rowan grabbed Alice's shoulder and guided her away from the scene, trying to be as quiet as possible. If Rhys was already turning into one of those things, he didn't want to be there when shit hit the fan.

The plan had displaced almost all of the motel guests through to the courtyard outside. The police were putting up a fight, but Rowan could hear the dwindling energy, the first utterances of defeat, voices calling for an evacuation or backup.

"We go in a minute. We only have one shot at this," Rowan said.

Alice nodded.

"I only have room for two people in my truck. If any of you don't have a vehicle, I'll come back for more."

Most of the group nodded. If they didn't have a way out, it was tough luck. He wasn't coming back for shit.

Alice's eyes were glued to one of the people outside: a slobbish-looking man, staring at the sky, bewildered and bloody.

"You know him?" Rowan asked.

Alice shook her head.

"Not really. He sat by me on the coach. I thought he'd got out."

There was a tinge of guilt to her words, but she didn't seem too cut up about it.

The man sniffed the air and darted in another direction, his flabby body jiggling with every pace. Alice broke eye contact and huddled behind Rowan.

Rowan gripped the handle on the side entrance door, which opened up just behind the parking lot. There wasn't anyone watching this door—or if there was, they were long gone. Rowan scouted the area, checking for anyone ready to attack. It was eerily quiet, but he waved the others out.

His truck was about a hundred metres away, just a quick dash if he could find a clear path. A growling roar thundered from somewhere to his right side. It wasn't going to be as easy as he wanted it to be.

The first scream turned into four crazed strangers careening towards him from multiple directions. He grabbed a loose brick from a small trash pile and counted down the seconds until the first one was ready to attack.

A teenage girl descended on him, a garbled roar spilling from her mouth. Rowan forced the butt of the brick into her face, crumpling her nose. Alice rushed forward, intercepting a middle-aged man with a burnt face and oozing blisters. She had a brick too, which she belted into his face. One of the boils splatted a spray of yellow gunk on impact, dripping down into the man's lips. Alice finished him off with another hit.

The elderly woman was finally lost for words, because someone was making a meal of her neck. Her husband was on the floor too. Rowan pondered: curiously, the disease didn't seem to be spreading as he had expected it to. People theorised it was spreading through bodily fluid, but he hadn't actually seen any of the victims turn yet. And many of the corpses with serious injuries weren't getting back up at all.

Alice launched her brick at a third assailant, choking his momentum and sending him crashing to the asphalt. It was a lucky shot, but it did the job. Now she was without a weapon. Rookie error. The final attacker careened into her back, wrestling her to the ground.

Face-down and crushed by the considerable weight on top of her, Alice was completely helpless. Seeing her like that, in need of assistance, flailing on the ground, was kind of hot in Rowan's mind. He could sweep in like Prince Charming, show her what a brave, charismatic gentleman he could be. And he did just that, ripping the person off by his hair, feeling the roots snap beneath his grasp. Rowan discarded him to the floor and stamped on the back of his neck until he stopped fighting.

"Come on," Rowan beamed, holding his hand out to Alice. She took it, just like the little damsel in distress she was. They jogged to the truck, avoiding any other confrontations. The keys rattled against the door as Rowan twisted the lock, quickly ushering Alice into the passenger seat. He crept around the back of the vehicle, checking everything was still connected and correctly secured.

He recoiled. An officer lay propped up against the back doors, most of his face missing. An exposed eyeball bulged from one of his sockets, the other gouged out, leaving a pulpy crevice. Most of the flesh on his face was shredded in tatters, revealing slick, raw muscle.

Somehow, this officer was still alive. He was stuck in place, reaching for his rifle, desperately ready to end it all.

"Do you want that?" Rowan asked.

The officer bent his neck round, staring at Rowan with that one contorted eyeball.

"Kill me," the officer choked, unable to speak properly. It was only then that Rowan realised he was missing his top lip too.

The chaos had dwindled down to just a few people and crazies, the fallen scattered across the tarmac. The silence had returned, and whatever was left of the motel group had returned inside. Rowan could hear cars screeching to escape, the rest of the visitors making a mad dash towards the block-ade. What they would find there would be anyone's guess, but by hanging back for a moment or two, Rowan could use any distraction to sail right through.

Rowan returned his focus to the disfigured officer.

"Please," the officer croaked, gesturing for his weapon.

People these days had no fight. They were weak-willed, ready to give up at every corner. Just like his wife. That bitch was a walking failure, blaming her troubles on anything external to waive her guilt. Rowan was the one making all the money, doing all the chores, trying to be intimate... It was never enough. So much so that when he'd rumbled her affair, *she* broke down crying. It was all about her feelings, her wants, her needs.

Selfish waste of space. His wife and the man in front of him were one and the same.

Rowan grabbed the rifle from the floor and considered it for a moment.

"Kill... me..." the faceless man mumbled, gasping in agony.

"That's it? You get into a fight and just give up?"

The police officer didn't quite have the face needed to make an expression, but something definitely shifted.

"P-lease."

Begging. Now we're onto begging.

"Rowan, hurry up!"

That was Alice, raring to go.

"One moment. I'm checking the wheels!"

Rowan stared back at the man.

"You're the ones who are meant to protect us."

He gobbed a snotty ball of saliva onto the officer's chest.

"Get up and do your job," Rowan spat, leaving the man behind, pleading for sweet release. He chucked the rifle into the middle seat, and climbed up ready to drive.

"What was that about?" Alice asked.

Rowan shook his head.

"Nothing. Let's go."

The vehicle stuttered into action and Rowan started to weave his way through bodies and broken car parts. The car park was narrow by design, and trying to control a vehicle of the truck's size was a thankless task. Even so, he managed to manoeuvre through the obstacles and get to the slip road.

"I can't see anything through the blood," Alice moaned, referencing the splatter on the windscreen.

Rowan switched the wipers on, releasing some fluid to scrub away the stain. Alice probably assumed it got messy in the violence. She didn't need to know about the stranded stranger he had used as target practice on the motorway. That was one of his little secrets.

Right up ahead, a miscellany of lights and sirens were stretched across all four lanes, with a smaller blockade to cut off the slip road. The cars that had left before them were parked up just before the block, unable to move forward or turn back.

Rowan wasn't going back inside that building. The gap between the vehicles ahead of him was barely wide enough to get a motorbike through, let alone a HGV. But with enough of a run-up to catch some speed and a burning desire for freedom, it was as tempting a plan as any.

"I think I have enough to get us to the outskirts," Rowan said, glaring at the fuel gauge on the dashboard.

"Anything is better than here," Alice answered. "What are you thinking?"

"You know the saying, if you can't go round it…"

"Are you sure? That doesn't sound too—" Alice started, but was not given a chance to finish.

Rowan compressed the accelerator. The truck churned, sparking to life. There was just enough distance between where they were and the barrier to reach 30mph, taking the slight downwards gradient into consideration.

The engine rumbled. Tree branches dragged across the top of the cab. In the trailer, stacks of pallets clattered together, various foodstuffs packed and ready for the supermarket. Half of it was frozen, likely spoiled now.

The scene in front of them of panicked drivers fleeing their cars rushed towards the windscreen. The front of the truck smashed into the first car, launching it to the side with a crumpled door. The others fired off like dominos. At escalating speed, Rowan broke through the cordon, running right over the poor bastard who was managing it too. There were too many crunchy things under the wheels, so he didn't get to enjoy the pop of that one.

"Fuck!" Alice screamed, but Rowan just kept accelerating. Fresh off the slip-road and on course to the motorway, there was just one more obstacle: a larger barrier, and soldiers with guns.

"Shit," Rowan exhaled.

But he welcomed the onslaught of bullets. In a spray of frantic gunfire, the bonnet lit up like a firework display, sparking with hot metal. Speed was on Rowan's side, so before any of the bullets hit their target, the truck was already ripping through the hastily-built fencing. The soldiers had the forethought to jump out of the way, at least. He could tell they survived by the sound of more bullets rattling off behind them.

The horizon was clear, no traffic or obstacles to hold them up now. It was a ten-minute journey to Egglemore, then they could put this all behind them.

Though, as he always liked to remind himself, a lot could happen in ten minutes.

CHAPTER 25
TODD

It was fucking freezing. Damp. Itchy.

Todd had woken up in the toilet cubicle a few hours ago, and had only just managed to make it out the door. His body was exhausted, but more than that, his mind was over-whelmed.

In the forest, things were still normal. Wildlife, trees and birdsong, a thriving circus of nature.

But out *there*, he needed a plan.

Snotty and irritable, Todd soldiered on. His jumpers provided next to no protection against the cold last night. He just thanked God and the universe that no-one had tried to come in and hurt him whilst he slept.

The carnage of the day before was playing on his mind, vibrant nightmares bleeding into his reality, tainting his every thought. He hadn't encountered a whole lot of death in his life: goldfish, pet dog, a distant relative. Yesterday was like living in a warzone, where the casualties were up close and personal, and included seeing your only family ravaged apart by a friendly neighbour.

A static pinch ran through his hamstring and lower back,

agonisingly sharp and uncomfortable. The aftershock of yesterday's events were catching up with him.

Todd slunk to the grass, leaning back against one of the oaks. If he'd had a few supplies and some proper shelter, he reckoned he could probably get used to this life for a bit. Unfortunately, he had zero survival skills, and if it wasn't for the serendipitous appearance of the toilet block, he'd have probably slept out on the forest floor and died of hypothermia. So he wouldn't get ahead of himself.

For the last few years, he'd barely ventured outside of a one square mile radius of his apartment. His only real friend lived out of town, and everything he needed—shops, restaurants, a very occasional cinema trip—were very close by. Faced with a complete shift from this way of life, Todd just wanted to cry and give up. But he wouldn't do that.

Uncertain if it even had any battery left, Todd pulled the drone, goggles, and controller from his backpack. The meter signalled he had enough power for a couple of hours in the sky. Trying to launch it from his current position would be a disaster waiting to happen, especially with the tightly-packed branches above. With a deep sigh, he grabbed his bags and took a breath, heading to the edge of the park to find some clear skies.

At least it wasn't raining now. He was still full of cold, achingly exhausted, but a little rested. After walking for ten minutes, he was on the edge of the main perimeter, and set the drone on a small electricity box. Moments later it was hovering in the air, and Todd had the goggles wrapped around his head. With the controls, he took it up high and started exploring the streets.

A fire burned inside one of the big supermarkets, smoke pluming from the entryway. Half a mile down the same road, a big group were fighting, striking a stranger with a miscellany of weapons. Whether he was one of those crazed people or it was just an opportunistic fight in the face of increasing lawlessness, it didn't fill Todd with much hope.

He tried to map out the area in his head. Two miles further in this direction would lead him to the docks. The ferry to Oasis Harbour usually ran like clockwork, four evenly-spaced time slots every day. He'd never taken the trip before, but the idea of jumping right into a scenario with tons of frustrated people trying to escape the city filled him with absolute dread.

He toggled the lever to spin the drone ninety degrees to the right and set upon a new path. A few bodies littered the floor, alongside strewn belongings and broken glass. Plenty of people seemed to be getting on with their day, despite the curfew. It was kind of crazy, the way that this *thing* seemed so widespread, yet people were still ignorantly walking around, socialising and hanging out.

A totalled police car blocked the entrance of one street, surrounded by a group of four or five of the deranged strangers. They were clawing at the windows, trying to get inside, smashing their faces off the glass. The contrast between one street and the next was considerable, pockets of violence playing out in plain sight.

Todd clicked a button on his controls, carefully watching the live view through the goggles. The drone descended smoothly, stopping when it was about six feet in the air. He wanted a view of the ground, to see if there was anything he might be missing. If he was going to venture out with little more than a couple of bags and a pocketful of hard mints, scoping out his route in advance was his only failsafe.

Things coasted along nicely for a moment, before the tinny alarm started to ring through a small speaker on the headset. Something had collided with the drone. But he was in the middle of an empty street, no cars flowing through in either direction.

That must mean the impact was behind it.

Fumbling, Todd spun the drone a hundred and eighty degrees, and was met with a snarling, blood-stained mouth, snapping directly at the camera. He jumped back, as if this was happening directly in front of him, and immediately withdrew from the stranger. With a simple flick, he directed the aircraft to ascend, climbing away from the threats at street level. If only Todd had a way to fly through the air above the streets, he might have just felt a little more at ease.

The drone continued to rise, and when it seemed like things were back on course and moving forward, one of the propellers clipped the edge of a tree and careened onto a small ledge a few floors up.

"Fuck!" Todd screamed, eyes blanketed by the visual of the grey sky above the camera. The headset flickered with a message at the bottom of the visible screen: *Vehicle out of range.*

"Shit, shit, shit."

A wild screech erupted in front of him, but the drone wasn't showing anything but the sky. No-one could be out on the ledge, it was barely a metre wide.

Which meant…

Todd ripped off the headset just in time to see a well-dressed businesswoman sprinting towards him, barely a stone's throw away. Her head was half-scalped, a mound of hair and ripped flesh dangling by her ear. She bobbed with every movement, owing to her having only one high heel still attached, a torn up foot intermittently taking her weight.

There wasn't enough time to move, so Todd went limp, allowing her to tackle him to the ground. Keeping loose ensured he didn't injure himself when he fell, and bought him an extra second to think. With her disgusting face just inches away from his, he extended his right arm, sweeping the ground for something to use as a weapon. His other hand was around her neck, forcing her putrid head towards the sky.

She snapped and snarled, her weight surprisingly heavy

for such a small frame. Her body convulsed, making it impossible to keep her in one place for long. Elbows and kneecaps jutted into Todd's flesh, pinched skin. He screamed in pain.

His wrist was red hot, fingers twisted around her neck in desperation. He needed to end this quickly. His strength, was flagging. But he wasn't going to give up.

No fucking way.

A second rush of adrenaline blasted away any panic he may have felt. When his fingers finally brushed against a heavy, rough rock, he let out an exasperated grunt and, with all of the strength he could muster, cracked her right in the temple. Her body went limp and she collapsed to the side.

Todd waited a moment, caught his breath, and then pushed her off him. His body hurt, but he was alive. He slowly climbed to his feet, brushed off his jeans, and grabbed his bags. With sharp focus, he tracked across his hands and arms, searching for any signs of a break in his skin. A cut, perhaps. A bite he hadn't felt.

Injuries caused his Gran to succumb to this illness, so he couldn't be too careful. After triple-checking his body, he was ready to get going.

He needed his drone to survive this shitshow, which meant he had to track down the ledge it was resting on.

"Shit," he mumbled, dragging his feet as he set upon the journey.

◼ ◼ ◼ ◼ ◼

Things had been uneventful. Aside from sweaty palms and a heart rate that felt alarmingly close to a cardiac arrest, the walk was manageable. The air was filled with screams and sirens, sure, but it was all in the distance. That's what Todd was telling himself, anyway.

He was tracking the exact same route he'd flown the drone, ensuring that he had the best chance of finding the building it had landed on. Todd was hoping that a closer proximity would allow him to regain control of the aircraft, but it still wouldn't connect. It was possible the receiver had been damaged in the collision.

The walk was taking longer than he expected, and the further he ventured into the city, the more uncertain he was about the way back. Not that he could really turn around right now, anyway. The buildings were all starting to look the same. He was starting to regret not flying lower the whole way, so he'd at least have some kind of visual cues to go off.

"Can you help me?"

A young girl, no more than thirteen or fourteen, was holding her wrist, a chunk of skin ripped right out of it. Blood was pouring from the laceration, pooling on the ground beneath her.

Todd stopped, unsure of what to say or do. He didn't have any medical supplies with him aside from a few ibuprofens. And if that was a bite—which it certainly looked like it was—he had a good idea of how this situation was going to end.

"I'm sorry, I don't have anything with me—"

The girl looked right past Todd and started squealing.

"That's him! That's the guy who attacked me!"

Todd turned to face the prospect of another fight: a shredded athlete kitted out in expensive gym gear. Huge chest. Biceps bigger than Todd's legs. It had to be a fucking joke.

Heavy footsteps revealed the girl wasn't staying around for support; she'd just left her problems with Todd.

Great.

Todd turned, sprinting in the other direction, adrenaline spent and pure, unadulterated fear taking its place. His bedroom fitness regime was no match for the hulk of a man behind him, who was quickly gaining ground.

"Fuck off!" Todd screamed desperately, trying to reason

with whatever human lived within this freak. Safe to say, he wasn't listening, and Todd was running out of options. Miraculously, he recognised the street in front of him from the drone footage. It was here he had dropped to street level, which meant the aircraft was hanging on one of the surrounding ledges.

With blurry vision from the vibration of his feet hitting the pavement, Todd scanned the area frantically. For the second time in as many minutes, the universe had thrown him a rope. There was only one building with a ledge, some kind of office block.

Only a dozen paces in front of the madman, Todd launched himself at the door, praying it would open. A scared looking woman jumped to her feet, almost falling from a glass reception desk.

"There's a curfew! You shouldn't be in here."

Todd slammed the door behind him, securing it with the twist-lock.

"There's people everywhere. What's going on?" Todd asked.

The woman tutted, looking him up and down, silently questioning why he had bags with him.

"Are you sure you're in the right place?"

The beastly athlete sprinted right past the building, growling as he chased another random victim. The sound roared through the windowpanes, echoing.

"No-one ever listens to these emergency announcements. No wonder it's chaos out there."

Todd cleared his throat, trying not to throw up from the sporadic burst of exercise he'd just had to endure.

"Well why are you here?" he spat, struggling to maintain his usual polite manner.

"*I* am the only person in this building. Someone needs to be here to keep the office safe."

Todd couldn't be bothered to argue.

"Well, trust me, I wish I was stuck at home instead of here, but I'm not staying. I just need my drone."

"Drone?" she asked.

"I was flying it and it fell onto your ledge."

"So you've been out there playing with a drone whilst you're meant to be at home?"

Todd stood upright, wary of her accusatory tone.

"As I said, I wish I was home but it's not safe there. I was using my drone to find somewhere to go. I won't be a moment."

Todd continued forwards, heading down a corridor to find the staircase.

"You can't just go up there!" she moaned, heels clip-clopping on the floor.

"I won't be a minute, I just said."

Todd's heart was in overdrive.

Four things you can see.

Three things you can hear.

Gran screaming as Benjamin tore her apart.

The cackle that spilled from her lips as she tried to do the same to me.

Todd grabbed the banister, ready to climb the staircase. A hand grabbed his arm sharply.

"I'll report you to the police."

Todd scowled, seething.

"I saw my Gran turn last night… into one of those *things*. I had no problem defending myself against her. I'd take you out in a heartbeat."

Despite his stony exterior, Todd was in pure panic mode. His brain was blank, some primal instinct taking the place of his conscious mind. He'd never threatened anyone once in his life, he questioned whether she might burst out laughing at his feeble attempt at looking brave.

But she didn't laugh. Instead, she snatched her arm away and sped down the hall, taking her seat in a passive aggressive strop. She glanced back very quickly, only meeting his eyes for a millisecond. Todd took his chance, stumbling up each step, trying not to trip on his bag. The first two floors didn't have the ledge, but the third did. Todd stepped into a small office, glass-walled and super modern. Some kind of meeting room, perhaps.

The window slid open smoothly, and Todd was able to grab the drone without having to climb out onto the ledge. Back downstairs, he was trying to figure out a way to get rid of the receptionist so he could hunker down in the building. It wasn't big, but there were toilets, a bathroom, and a kitchen spread across the floors. It would be the perfect place to spend the night.

But who was he fooling? She wouldn't leave without a fight, and he was all out of energy for that.

So he walked back down the corridor and into the reception area. The woman behind the desk refused to make eye contact with him, so he just unlocked the door and left. The streets were a hive of activity, somehow full of dozens more people. Before Todd could make sense of the situation, an ambulance darted right towards the crowd from the other direction, swerving into the frontage of the shop opposite. The glass window imploded on impact, launching a rain of glass onto the pavement. Todd couldn't see if anyone was caught up in the crash, but the wave of people overflowing from the street to the middle of the road was alarming.

The hospital was just around the corner. He hadn't noticed the alarms before, but could they have been running from there? Todd was familiar with Egglemore Hospital, having joined his Gran at appointments every now and then. It was a super hospital, the only one in the county, and if all of these people were having to evacuate, how were they going to deal with all the new injuries? And what had caused it to get this bad?

People were yelling nonsense at him on their way past,

swerving to avoid him at the last moment. As if caught in a tornado, they were hurtling forth with no control of their bodies, just pure survival instinct.

Todd swallowed hard, his mouth dry, desperate for some water. He had only grabbed a half-full bottle from the flat when he packed his bag, and hadn't succeeded in making it last. He'd find a shop soon, but right now, he needed to get back inside.

He turned, smacking his hand against the door to the building he'd just left. The woman had locked him out, raising her eyebrows in disapproval.

"Let me back in! Please!"

Todd had lost whatever assertive exterior he'd had moments before. He pleaded to be let inside like a dog in the cold. The woman didn't move from her desk, breaking eye contact to read something on her phone.

"Shit! Fuck you!"

Todd jogged to the corner of the street, working his way against the crowd. The fact he was in the middle of the road didn't register until the car struck him, launching him from his feet into a crumple a few feet in front of the bonnet.

The vehicle wasn't going particularly fast before it hit him, but he'd still caught a decent amount of airtime before being reunited with the asphalt. Through blurry eyes, he saw an old Ford Focus with both front doors open. A large woman with shoulder-length ginger hair. He couldn't discern any of her facial features before losing consciousness.

The last thing he remembered was being frantically hauled into the car. He thought he may have hit his head, but it didn't hurt at all, didn't even make much of a sound.

The darkness was comforting. He wanted to stay a while.

CHAPTER 26

ROWAN

"Wait, Rowan."

Rowan looked at Alice across the cab, confused, before staring back at the road. The splintered windscreen was providing less and less visibility. He needed to get to the supermarket to make his delivery, and sort out a plan.

"I have signal. Can we stop so I don't lose it?"

Alice was practically out the door before Rowan even had a chance to pull over. He'd parked up in an industrial estate, which was concerningly devoid of any life. Alice slammed the door behind her and paced over to a wall, turning to lean against it. She was typing frantically on her phone.

Rowan pulled out his own device, connecting it to the on-board charger. As soon as the signal bars appeared on the screen, he swiped to the home security app. The picture was glitchy and intermittent, but finally settled. His wife was ghost-pale, slumped into a contorted position, urine pooling around her feet. The silly bitch was still trying to scream, her words whispering out in barely audible croaks.

The sound of knocking roared through the tinny speakers, coming from something out of range of the security camera.

Rowan quickly checked that Alice was still absorbed in her texting outside the truck, and returned to focus on the app.

Unable to help himself, he toggled on the speaker, and smiled as his lips pursed to speak.

"Are you behaving, kitten?"

His wife slowly arched to face the camera, and just began to scream, the vigour returning to her vocal cords. She bawled until she ran out of breath, quickly inhaled, and repeated the same thing several times. Her eyes were unwavering and unblinking.

Rowan's skin was tingling with beautiful sensations. It was pure fear in his wife's eyes, a bubbling pit of despair rising to consume her. The knowledge that this was the end, and it would be completely agonising until the final breath, was pure arousal to Rowan.

Ultimately, Rowan was extremely thankful for the cellular signal reconnecting. The gift of this shared moment, his wife's end and his new beginning, out of the shackles of that torturous life was something he would treasure always. The dream of a wife, two kids, and a great career was nothing more than a mirage, a stupid illusion created to pretend ordinary people could have a fairytale fantasy. Real life was lies, deceit, violence, and putting yourself first, taking what you could along the way. That was his mantra from now on. No more putting anyone before himself. No more selling himself short. If he wanted something, he would damn well get it.

The rattling on his phone grew louder. His wife ripped her eyes away from the camera and to the staircase. A frantic stranger tore onto screen, stumbling directly into the wall, before turning his sights on the bound woman in the middle of the room. The high angle shot captured the entire breadth of the space, allowing Rowan to watch the action and his wife's blood-curdling reaction to the situation.

Without any hesitation at all, the random man in Rowan's basement sprinted over to his wife, before stumbling back into a workbench. He tripped over boxes, feverishly flailing like a bird trying to escape through a small window. Finally, he started to babble some indecipherable shit, and slammed his interlocked fists into his wife's face. She convulsed, twisting at her restraints, blood dripping from her mouth.

Crouching into a contorted squat, the man was inches away from his wife's face. He was scratching his cheek, nails tearing against the skin, an insufferable itch burrowed deep inside his flesh. He continued to gargle nonsense, watching the blood drip from his wife with fascination.

Then, he interlocked his hands again, swung them back and cracked them into her forehead. This time, her cranium split with a juicy squelch. The blunt trauma coupled with the pillar behind her head seemed to have forced the pressure up through her skull, revealing her mangled interior. Rowan couldn't see much of the detail, but the pure sloppy joy radiating through the speaker was almost orgasmic. Never had revenge been served in such a deliciously visceral way.

Alice opened the door. Rowan locked his phone screen just in time. He didn't want to make a bad impression, not this early in a blossoming relationship. He was newly single, after all, a widower with a sob story ready-prepared and enough charisma to break through to any woman he desired. Alice rated pretty high on his list already, and the way she looked in those tight jeans wasn't changing his first impression.

"Let's go," she ordered, her attitude teetering on rudeness. Rowan loved a feisty woman, especially one that didn't quite know her place yet. He'd soon mould her into shape, let her take the lead for a while, see how things developed. He had a hotel room lined up for his overnight shift, a day of rest between deliveries. Though he was technically running at least twelve hours late, the order would still have to be delivered before he got off the clock.

But when he did, Alice would probably need somewhere

to stay. He only had one room, and she didn't seem to have anything lined up aside from a meeting. It would be the perfect occasion to really get to know each other, in a more up close and personal way. They could share a room. Share a bed. Maybe much more than that.

He could hardly wait to get his hands on her.

Any initial optimism for the rest of the afternoon was quickly quashed. On the way into the centre of Egglemore, they'd already seen two upturned vehicles, police vans called in from neighbouring counties, and soldiers sweeping the streets. Alice was restless in the passenger seat, shouting at her phone sporadically, lamenting the glitchy signal and lack of response from whoever she was texting.

Rowan wanted to know whom she was speaking to. He was curious, and her complete attachment to her phone told him that whatever she was talking about, it was important. He'd let her tell him in her own time. Maybe when they'd finally settled, she'd loosen up a bit.

Keeping to the wide lanes that ran the perimeter of the city's network of roads, Rowan spotted the turning to the supermarket he was due to deliver to. The road was surprisingly clear, so he coasted down in no time at all and took a right into the access lane at the rear of the building. The loading bay was about halfway up the lane, which was particularly narrow and had barely any room to swing the vehicle round. Worse still, a group of enraged shoppers were looting overturned baskets of groceries, everything from fresh meat to bottled water. An abandoned delivery van had already been combed through, yet people were still fighting for scraps.

A car had pulled in right behind the HGV, blocking Rowan from reversing out. This was a bad situation to be in, and he didn't have any immediate ideas on how to get out of it. Alice had just clocked the situation too, leaning forward to glance at the wing mirror.

A few particularly rowdy looters had already descended on the truck, wielding baseball bats and metal racking from the delivery van. Others were carting off trolley-loads of product to their vehicles in the adjacent parking lot, stuffing their boots with as many things as they could find. It was pure pandemonium, with the threat of real danger building in intensity.

They reached the HGV, and one man was already stabbing at the front tyres with a kitchen knife. Rowan adjusted in his seat, ready to get out, but Alice grabbed his wrist.

"Don't," she warned, her voice fragile and cold. She was concerned for her safety as much as Rowan's, and wasn't going to let him out without a fight.

"I can't go backwards," Rowan hissed, quickly running out of any options.

The twat in front of the vehicle was striking the knife down with all of his might, determined to puncture the tyre. Barely a minute later, he'd succeeded, celebrating with a slew of cocky gestures and a round of applause from his lackeys.

Rowan grabbed the gearstick and compressed the accelerator, reversing the vehicle as quickly as possible. The car behind them sounded their horn, but it quickly cut off when the trailer smashed into its bonnet.

Switching into first gear, Rowan slammed on the accelerator, forcing the crowd to back up.

"Rowan, be careful—"

The front of the truck smashed into the yob with the knife, sending him sprawling to the ground. He just about managed to worm his way to the side of the road, missing a sticky death by mere inches. The speed started to build, ready to flatten the looters into a paper-thin tapestry of guts and gore.

On a direct course to steamroll them all, the group were

saved by a stray hammer thrown at Rowan's windscreen, causing the corner to shatter in on his face. A stray fragment sliced his cheek, causing him to accidentally pull the steering wheel to the left, plummeting towards a solid metal shutter.

"Hold on!" Rowan screamed, unable to correct his mistake. The cab smashed against the shutter, causing the metal to fold inwards and snap off its mechanism. Rowan forced all his weight onto the brake, but the vehicle continued to skid. He had no control.

The left side of the truck scraped the edge of the bay, rough brick scratching away the fading white paintwork. The brake was completely useless, and he had barely a second of conscious thought before the entire vehicle careened into a wall. Alice's head hit the dashboard. Rowan took a sharp breath before his mind faded to black.

CHAPTER 27

MAGGIE

Shit shit shit.

Claire grabbed one of the kid's arms, and Maggie heaved his body up to balance on her shoulder. He looked about early twenties, tall, with mousy brown hair. They quickly slid him into the backseat, and Claire slammed the door shut. His bags were strewn on the road, so Maggie quickly scooped them up and dumped them in the passenger seat. A backpack and a duffle bag. Some kind of drone was visible through the broken zip.

"Is he okay?" Maggie asked, releasing the handbrake. He'd appeared out of nowhere, right in the middle of the road. The car was hardly going twenty miles an hour, but he'd still flown a good few metres through the air.

She could hardly catch a break today. She just kept hurting people.

A crowd was blocking the entire street. Maggie noticed a few of them from the hospital, still mindlessly looking for a way out, just like she was. Her and Claire had already tried a shortcut out of the city, but every direction had some kind of obstacle. She could take the motorway and track around some country lanes to get back to her home in Longsville, but it added an extra hour and plenty of treacherous roads to the journey.

The direct route, the one she'd taken in, was diverted through a zig-zag of residential roads, and things were at a near standstill.

"We need to get him to a doctor!" Claire moaned, trying to keep him upright in the back. He was conscious, just about, but slurring his words and unable to keep his head balanced.

"Well, we can't go back there!" Maggie replied, sounding more panicked than she would have liked.

She needed to keep calm. They were getting out of there. Just a couple of miles and they were set. Maggie beeped the horn, but the sound went largely unnoticed by the stream of people in front of her.

Out of ideas, she revved the engine loud, and the entire vehicle lurched forwards.

"Sorry," Maggie said under her breath, apologising to the sputtering car and its deteriorating vintage. Thankfully, the crowd seemed to part, merging back to the footpath. In the chaos, there was at least some order. The streets swept past as Maggie hit the accelerator, cutting up a roundabout and darting into a small lane. The coast was clear from here on out.

Or it seemed to be that way until another mile down the road, where a cordon of some kind had been erected. As she coasted closer to the scene, however, she noticed that the fencing was completely obliterated. Two people were lifeless on the floor, and another one was stalking the grassy mound to the side of the road. His mannerisms were random, forced. Blood stained his mouth and chest, uniform torn into a shredded net.

Maggie picked up speed again, and roared through the gap in the blockade, taking little notice of the speed limit or the flash of multiple speed cameras on the way.

They'd be safe at home soon. Then they could find a doctor for this kid, and lock down the property to keep all of this far away from them. She couldn't rest until they were there.

CHAPTER 28

CHARLES

Charles was glowing from his second hot shower in as many days. Draped in some clothes that belonged to Olive's ex-boyfriend, and were easily two sizes too large, he had been tempted into another glass of Zinfandel, and had already downed half.

Inside the apartment, things seemed cosy. Secure. He'd never dream of getting used to being there—there was a difference between a lucky day and a miracle—but whilst he had the chance, Charles was determined to make the most of it.

Olive returned to the living room from her own shower, a dressing gown wrapped loosely around her body. She glugged the remnants of a third or fourth glass of wine, and prepared another right after.

"So, what's the plan now?" Olive asked playfully.

"Well I'd love a good sleep. I haven't had a bed in a while."

The words came out sadder than he had expected. Though the streets were as far from comfortable as you could imagine, he'd never felt particularly overwhelmed by his situation. It was a fact of life, just like breathing and having to empty your bladder. The scales of fate teetered in both directions. Sometimes you win, sometimes you lose.

"The guest room is all set up. I'm going to do some stuff for a while, but please feel free to lay down whenever you want to."

Charles nodded warmly.

"And then?" Charles asked. "What's our plan?"

Olive straightened, resting on the side of the sofa opposite.

Hesitantly, she cupped her hands together, looking as if she wanted to ask something, but too afraid to let it out.

Instead, she turned on the TV, and suggested taking a look at the local news.

"*Egglemore is in its second day of a citywide lockdown. Curfews are running twenty-four hours a day, with only a few exceptions.*"

The woman on TV was the same one presenting the segment the day before, when he'd watched it at the café. Charles didn't get too much of a chance to watch TV, so he wasn't familiar with her work, but he presumed that she was always on at this time.

"*Contactless food delivery is running on a reduced schedule due to stock issues. All convenience stores have been ordered to close or run on a severely reduced schedule. Latest reports say that Egglemore Hospital has declared an emergency. All emergency services are being rerouted to facilities outside of the city.*"

They finished watching the segment and switched off the TV. Charles finished his wine, and slapped his hands on his knees, politely signalling his intention to get to bed.

"I have a question to ask you... well, more of a favour," Olive said.

"Okay," Charles agreed, "Go ahead."

She stood up, walking over to rest on the edge of the sofa Charles was occupying.

"I need you to promise not to freak out."

Charles nodded, concerned at what was coming.

"I have something really important I need to do, and I need your help to do it."

Charles didn't love the sound of this, but he continued to listen, nevertheless.

"Firstly, I need your help getting to my holiday home. I'm meeting someone there and it's imperative I don't miss it."

"How can I help with that?" Charles asked.

"I'll explain," she said, "but there's something more pressing, too."

Olive stood up, her eyes scanning the floor, avoiding his eye contact. Eventually, she swallowed hard, grabbing the shoulder of her dressing gown.

"Secondly, I need your help with this."

She pulled down the fabric around her right shoulder, revealing a gaping bite wound, already tinged with pockets of infection.

Charles recoiled, breath snatched from his lungs.

"You're… bit?"

Olive did a slow sarcastic clap.

"The good news is I won't become one of them."

Charles sank back into the sofa, suddenly wary of the space he'd got himself trapped in. He knew he shouldn't have had that wine.

"What makes you so sure?" Charles asked hesitantly.

"You're not going to let me go to sleep," she said matter-of-factly.

They stared at each other for a short moment.

"What do you mean? You said you were staying up a bit."

"I'm staying up all night. I've got no choice."

Charles chuckled, mostly because he had no other idea how to react. Was this all a prank?

"You want me to keep you awake? Why?" he asked, a slight annoyance in his tone.

"Because if I go to sleep, I become one of them. If I don't, well, I won't."

Charles shook his head, completely clueless as to what she was trying to convey.

"I'm sorry. I don't know what you're talking about."

Olive walked right up to him, and crouched to look him in the eyes.

"I really need to get to that building tomorrow," she said, talking a million miles an hour. "I can't explain everything now, but I know what's happening here. I know how this all plays out, I know the scenarios, and I know how this disease works. If you're bitten, scratched, share any bodily fluids, you're infected. The incubation period is from that moment until you sleep. You really can't let me sleep, not even for a moment."

Charles stood up and scratched his head, trying to decide on a next move.

"If what you're saying is true, and I highly doubt it isn't, you mean that when you finally can't stay awake any longer—"

Olive sighed deeply.

"—then I need someone I can trust to take care of me. Take me out."

"I don't know if I'm that guy," Charles said, trying to make sense of what she was saying.

"I'm afraid we've got no other choice. Don't let me go to sleep."

Sirens echoed outside, and Charles was suddenly more uncomfortable than he had been in a long time. He was living with a ticking time bomb, and if he dared take his eye off of her for even ten minutes, it could be game over.

Charles needed to get the fuck out of this city.

The end.

Continue the series with 'Dead Awake: Overrun' on Amazon.

Stay Awake. Stay Informed.

Enjoying *Dead Awake*? Don't miss what's coming next. Sign up to my **horror email community** to:

- Get exclusive *bonus scenes and behind-the-scenes lore* from the world of *Dead Awake*.
- Be the first to know when the next book in the series is live.
- Get special offers and news on my other original horror releases

The infection's spreading fast — don't fall asleep on the series.

Click here to join now.

See you on the other side…

Printed in Dunstable, United Kingdom